RIDING FOR AMERICA

Riding for America

Nancy Hays

NANCY HAYS ENTERTAINMENT, INC.

www.nancyhaysentertainment.com

Contents

Forward from Nancy Hays   x

A Note to the Reader: Chronological Order   xi

1   America - 1860 - Jerry's Long Journey   1

2   America - 1861 - Birth Record   4

3   Isaac - 1879 - Early Morning, August in New York   8

4   Isaac - 1879 - Travers Stakes at Saratoga   11

5   America - 1864 - Back at the Tanner Farm   17

6   America - 1864 - Observation and Intuition   21

7   America - 1864 - Slave Quarter Tension   23

8   America - 1864 - A Trip to the Marketplace   27

9   Isaac - 1879 - Isaac, Up Before the Roosters   31

10   Isaac - 1879 - The Unpleasant Train Car Ride   34

11   Isaac - 1881 - Chester Park Race Day Scuffle   36

12   Isaac - 1881 - Suspended   40

13   Isaac - 1881 - Talk of Snapper   43

14   America - 1864 - Boots Brings News   44

15   America - 1864 - Last Night at the Tanner Farm   47

16   America - 1864 - America Says Goodbye   48

17   America - 1864 - First Light   50

18   America - 1864 - Morning on the Outskirts   51

19 America - 1864 - Milly and Louisa   52

20 America - 1864 - Camp Nelson Refugees   55

21 America - 1864 - Isaac Meets His Father   56

22 America - 1864 - Onward to Battle   59

23 America - 1864 - Back in the Barracks   60

24 America - 1864 - Cast into the Woods   63

25 America - 1864 - Freezing in the Forest   65

26 Isaac - 1881 - Isaac Meets Lucy at Craw Bottom   69

27 Isaac - 1883 - Nuptials and Honeymoon Train   73

28 America - 1865 - Refugee Rescue   75

29 America - 1865 - Warm Welcome at the Jordans   78

30 America - 1865 - Time Passes at the Jordans   81

31 America - 1865 - A New Day in the USA   82

32 America - 1865 - Fort Nelson News   85

33 America - 1865 - Staying Strong   88

34 America - 1869 - Solar Eclipse, August 7   90

35 Isaac - 1884 - The First American Derby   93

36 Isaac - 1884 - Racing in the Windy City   95

37 Isaac - 1884 - Lucky Makes an Entrance   97

38 Isaac - 1885 - Second American Derby   101

39 Isaac - 1886 - Isaac's Dreams for His Future   102

40 Isaac - 1886 - Charles and the Shakespeare Play   104

41 Isaac - 1886 - An Unexpected Encounter   107

42 Isaac - 1887 - Isaac's History Making Contract   110

43 Isaac - 1887 - The Superstar   112

44 Isaac - 1887 - Mansion Dreams in Lexington   114

45 Isaac - 1889 - At the Cigar Club   116

46 Isaac - 1889 - At the Haggin Mansion   118

47 Isaac - 1889 - One Star Meets Another 120

48 America - 1870 - Inspiration from Literature 122

49 America - 1872 - Freedman's Bank Deposit 125

50 America - 1872 - A New Job Offer 126

51 America - 1872 - Williams Manor and Stables 129

52 Isaac - 1890 - Weighing In, Curbing Hunger 130

53 Isaac - 1890 - A Photographic Marvel 132

54 Isaac - 1890 - A Newsman for the Ages 136

55 Isaac - 1890 - The Match Race of the Century 139

56 Isaac - 1890 - Haggin Mansion Celebration 142

57 Isaac - 1890 - Stables by Night 149

58 Isaac - 1890 - What's in that Drink? 151

59 Isaac - 1890 - Manmouth Racetrack 152

60 Isaac - 1890 - A Fever Dream and Pain 156

61 America - 1874 - Freedman's Bank Demise 159

62 America - 1875 - Confrontation and Persuasion 162

63 America - 1875 - Williams' Stables, Morning 165

64 Isaac - 1891 - A Special Visitor with News 168

65 Isaac - 1891 - A Young Admirer 171

66 Isaac - 1891 - The Big Party for a Best Friend 173

67 Isaac - 1891 - An Engagement Party for the Ages 175

68 Isaac - 1891 - Forgiveness 178

69 Isaac - 1896 - Vivid Memories 181

70 Isaac - 1896 - The End is Near 187

71 Isaac - 1896 - A Funeral for a Prince 188

72 America - 1879 - African Cemetery No. 2 190

73 America - 1879 - Saturday at Saratoga 192

Definitions and Historical Information 196

America and Isaac Murphy's Legacy and Inspiration 243

Study Guide 247

RIDING FOR AMERICA

A young adult novel by Nancy Hays, adapted from a screenplay by
Eddie and Nancy Heffernan

BASED ON A TRUE STORY

Forward from Nancy Hays

From the moment I first read about Isaac Murphy's remarkable career and winning percentage during a visit to the Kentucky Derby Museum in 2019, I knew his journey was the story of a great American sports hero. After viewing the exhibit, I pored over *The Prince of Jockeys*, a historical biography by distinguished professor of African American history Pellom McDaniels III, as well as *I Dedicate This Ride*, a book of poetry by Frank X Walker, and *Race Horse Men* by Katherine C. Mooney. I was captivated.

I also studied the work of those who have tried to piece together the factual details of Isaac Murphy's life and the broader American context in which he lived. Even with all the existing archives, much remains unknown—and much of what is known is inconsistent. Due to missing records and distorted accounts by those who sought to downplay Isaac's accomplishments because of prejudice and racism, writing a novel about his life posed an added layer of complexity.

Because this book is historical fiction, exact chronology of race dates have been altered and some characters were created for the story and are not based on historical figures. However, the real historical characters are deeply woven into the narrative, and their legacy is undeniable. I hope the conversations readers encounter between characters feel authentic to the time. The goal is to honor the legacy of the greatest American sports icon of the 19th century.

I am thrilled to share Isaac Burns Murphy's story with a new generation of sports enthusiasts and to educate readers about the true history of Thoroughbred horse racing in America—and the foundational role African American jockeys played in its beginnings. After all, history must set the record straight. Thank you for reading and sharing.

A Note to the Reader: Chronological Order

Riding for America is a dual narrative, intertwining two stories: America's and Isaac's. Photography and illustrations are included to help the reader distinguish between the two timelines. From the start, we wanted readers to understand the powerful relationship between mother and son—beginning with young Isaac's early years and continuing up to age eighteen—and the significant role his mother played in shaping his life and career.

1

America - 1860 - Jerry's Long Journey

The night was still and the moon full. The year was 1860. It was quiet in the slave quarters on the outskirts of Lexington, Kentucky, at the Tanner farm. Jerry Burns, a field hand with a penchant for playful mischief, pressed his ear gently against the belly of his pregnant wife, America Murphy. America was softer and more cautious than Jerry, with eyes that watched, observed, and analyzed everything around her.

"I hear him! He's kicking, sayin', 'Lemme out! Lemme out!'" Jerry whispered, close to America's ear.

America laughed quietly and shushed him. In the dimness, Jerry lifted his head slightly to glance around at the other men and women sleeping on wooden pallets within the cramped confines of the quarters.

"You keep sayin' 'him,'" Jerry teased with a grin.

"It's a boy. I know it's a boy," America whispered back. "I had an appetite like a hungry boy—cravin' beans more than usual, which is what you like and I don't. And I keep gigglin' for no good reason. Maybe this one's gonna be funny like you."

"But it kicks," Jerry said.

America looked puzzled. "What's that mean?"

"You kick," Jerry teased.

"I do not," she replied, indignant.

"Sure you do," he chuckled, squeezing her gently under the arm.

She flinched and kicked at him, trying not to laugh.

"See? Told you!" Jerry whispered, triumphant.

There was a stirring nearby. America quickly shushed him again. Their eyes met in the low light, full of warmth and joy despite the harshness of their world.

"Boy or girl, I just hope the little one learns how to whisper," America murmured.

Jerry leaned in close to her ear. "I can whisper."

They lay there for a moment in silence. But something shifted in America's eyes. Her expression turned serious.

"Jerry, you best go. I don't want you caught up in the trouble of the night."

"I know the way, America. Let me stay a little longer."

"If you stay too late, you'll tire yourself out."

"I don't get tired. Not when it comes to seein' you."

"It's enough you sneak away as it is."

"It's only ten miles."

"That's ten miles too far."

"America… I ain't ever get to see you long enough…" Jerry's voice caught.

America lifted his head gently with her hand. "I love you, Jerry. And there's no need to say 'ain't.'"

"Well, my deepest apologies, missus," Jerry said with a smile. "But I ain't leavin' 'til you fall asleep. Both of you."

America closed her eyes and pretended to sleep. Jerry, still wide awake, lay quietly by her side. After several long minutes, he slowly pulled his hand from beneath her and rose from the pallet.

At the door, Jerry slipped into a thick sack coat and patched hat. Through the frosted window, he could see the snow swirling over the dark, barren fields.

He pulled a small flask from his coat, took a quick swig to calm his nerves, and stepped silently out into the cold night.

Back in bed, America opened her eyes. She had been watching him go, her heart heavy with love and worry.

2

America - 1861 - Birth Record

Jenny, a fourteen-year-old girl with skinny legs, long black hair, and dark brown skin, worked alongside America on the Tanner farm. She helped with laundry, house cleaning, and polishing the silver for Master and Missus Tanner.

Like many teenage girls, Jenny was giddy and sometimes impulsive, but she knew better than to show it while working inside the Tanner home. It was considered a privilege to serve as a house slave, rather than laboring in the hot tobacco fields. Jenny was determined not to be reassigned. She watched America closely, treating her as both a mentor and an example—America was not only literate, but a perfectionist when it came to cleaning. She was sharp-minded and intuitive.

America had a talent for reading people and situations. It was almost as if she could anticipate what others were thinking or were about to do. The Tanners valued her highly—she was the best domestic worker on the farm and the one who kept the household in order. On a frigid January night in 1861, Jenny would become the first to announce America and Jerry's new arrival.

"That's it, America!" Jenny shouted, her voice rising in excitement. She sat beside America in the slave quarters, dabbing her forehead with a cloth and holding a bucket of water nearby.

Next to her was Sarah, a proud, nurturing Black woman in her forties. As America writhed and moaned through labor, Sarah stood over her, guiding the delivery with calm authority. Jenny, momentarily distracted by the birth, dabbed absentmindedly at America's nose instead of her forehead.

"Pay 'tention and cool her head, Jenny," Sarah said firmly.

"Breathe now, America," Jenny whispered. "Baby's almost here."

"Hold on now. Here we go… baby's comin'!" Sarah coached.

America screamed one last time and gave a final push.

A few minutes later, a newborn baby's cries echoed softly through the quarters. Sarah swaddled the infant in an apron and a thin bed cloth, then placed him gently in America's arms. Exhausted, her breath visible in the cold air, America rested her head against the tiny boy and whispered his name: "Isaac."

Jenny, overwhelmed with joy, grabbed a lantern in one hand and lifted her skirt with the other. She raced across the snowy fields toward the big white farmhouse.

At the porch, she was met by Deacon, the Tanners' butler—a tall, gentle man in his forties with a kind face etched with deep worry and quiet strength.

"America alright?" he asked.

"Yes! She's tired, but she's alright—and the baby's here!" Jenny beamed.

Deacon opened the heavy front door and let her in, holding a finger to his lips as a signal to keep her voice down. They made their way toward the library to deliver the news to David Tanner.

David Tanner, a White man in his late forties, sat in a large armchair before a roaring fire. Spectacled and always appearing severe, he had the air of someone who had never known joy. He was raised as a proper Southern gentleman, and his vast personal library reflected his bookish, rigid nature.

Deacon approached and spoke gently. "Mr. Tanner, sir?"

There was a pause. Tanner remained turned away.

"A moment…" he muttered.

After another pause, Tanner finally responded.

"Yes, what is it?"

Before Deacon could speak, Jenny blurted out, "America had her baby, sir!"

Tanner smacked his lips and slowly turned his chair.

"Ah. I was wondering when that would happen. Both healthy?"

"Yes, sir," Jenny answered quickly.

"Well, glad to hear it." Tanner rubbed his shoulder and pulled his blanket tighter. "It's plumb cold in here. Jenny, fetch the poker—I want to stir these embers. Deacon, get me the manifest—second drawer."

"Yes, sir," Deacon replied, moving to retrieve the ledger.

"The baby," Jenny tried again, "his name is—"

Tanner interrupted. "Didn't hear much screaming," he murmured. "When Margaret had Emma, she screamed so loud I'm sure bonnets flew off heads in Timbuktu. If they wear bonnets there."

A rare smile played on his lips.

Deacon smiled faintly as he handed over the manifest.

Jenny tried again, more urgently. "The baby's name, sir, it's—"

Tanner ignored her. "Today's the sixth, right?"

"I believe so, sir," Deacon answered.

"Good." Tanner dipped a quill into the inkwell, opened the ledger to the "Property" section, and used his finger to find the correct entry. He wrote carefully: "1 boy."

Then, scanning the page, he frowned.

"Deacon, those hogs—I have four listed here. There were only three in the pen last I checked."

"Yes, sir. The fourth died about a week ago, Master Tanner."

Tanner sighed. "Next time, remind me to write it down."

"I thought I did, sir, but I could be mistaken."

"No, you didn't. This will have to be amended."

"Yes, Master Tanner. My apologies."

Jenny tried once more, her voice quiet but determined. "The baby's name is—"

But Tanner snapped the ledger shut and turned his chair back toward the fire. "That's all I need to know, girl. Hurry along now, Deacon. Get the poker. I'm cold."

Jenny stood still, her eyes on the fire. Then, quietly, almost to herself, she whispered, "Isaac."

3

Isaac - 1879 - Early Morning, August in New York

Isaac Murphy, Keeneland Library Hemment Collection

Eighteen years had passed, and Isaac was now a handsome young man. It was a beautiful summer day in upstate New York. Isaac sat on a bench in a stable stall, reading a hard-bound book. He finished a chapter, slipped the book into a satchel, and walked into the main barn, heading toward a specific horse's stall. He approached the stall quietly, careful not to startle the animal. Leaning his head against the muzzle of a sleek chestnut Thoroughbred, he gently smoothed the horse's hide, whispering to it softly.

Still and confident, Isaac radiated a quiet strength. He was unmistakably America Murphy's son. He bore her features—and her intellect and dignity. Clad in green and white racing silks, he carried himself with the unassuming grace that would soon earn him the nickname, the "Prince of Jockeys."

The stable door swung open, and in walked Eli Jordan—a Black man in his fifties dressed in a tailored coat, silver pocket watch glinting, and a brass-handled cane in hand. He moved with the calm command of a seasoned racehorse trainer, a man who had earned his stature.

Eli walked straight up to Isaac and said, "It's time."

"He knows," Isaac replied, patting the horse. "He knows it's race day."

"Well, that's good. But it don't matter much what he knows," Eli said, locking eyes with Isaac. "What matters now is what he does."

Eli nodded to Edward West, a young stable hand of eleven years, who took the reins from Isaac and began to lead the horse from the stall.

"Don't make him too comfortable, Isaac," Eli warned. "He has to understand he's not the favorite."

Isaac grinned. "He's the favorite in my book."

Eli looked directly into Isaac's eyes again. "He's gotta want it, Ike."

"I know, Eli," Isaac replied. "I talked to him. He wants it."

Eli tilted his head slightly. "And what about you?"

"Me?" Isaac smirked. "Saratoga's a big stage."

He swept his arm as if performing for an audience, then quoted Shakespeare with a playful air: "All the world's a stage, Eli. I'm a mere player."

Eli raised his eyebrows. "You nervous?"

Isaac's eyes narrowed. "It's my first major Stakes race. I didn't sleep a wink last night. And I'm riding against Spendthrift. I think I'm allowed to be a little nervous."

"You remember what I told you about ridin' with emotion?" Eli asked.

Isaac nodded. "Use it, right?"

Edward returned with the horse. Isaac stepped up, swung into the saddle with practiced ease, and settled in.

"Don't let it use you," Eli warned.

4

Isaac - 1879 - Travers Stakes at Saratoga

The grandstand at Saratoga Park was a sight to behold on race day for the famed Travers Stakes. The upstate New York air was crisp, and the crowd gathered beneath wide green awnings, abuzz with anticipation. The wealthiest attendees came dressed in their finest—ladies in colorful hats with wide brims, men in tailored suits—ready to cheer their horses to victory and flaunt their fortunes with wagers large enough to turn heads.

Among the well-to-do were everyday folks too—dockworkers, servants, cooks—each hoping for a miracle bet that might earn them more than a week's wages. All around the grandstand, small bills and coins changed hands. Notes were scribbled in makeshift journals. Last-minute bets were shouted through windows. The energy was electric.

Along the rails stood Porter and Winston, two young White men in their twenties, dockhands who were grizzled with work. They spit tobacco and argued over picks.

"Twenty cents on Spendthrift," Porter said, confidently. "You'd be dumber than a sack of rocks to pick otherwise."

"I'm tellin' you, my Aunt Jessie jammed her pinky last week and can't play piano no more," Winston barked. "That's why I'm goin' with Maestro."

"Ha! If music's all ya got, why not pick Falsetto, you lazy foozler?" Porter fired back.

"Well... who's ridin' Falsetto?" Winston asked.

"Don't matter who the damn jockey is," Porter replied through a mouthful of chew. "It's the horse that matters."

Standing nearby was Ben, a Black man in his late thirties, with his twelve-year-old son, Joshua. Ben overheard the conversation and interjected calmly, "Name's Isaac Burns Murphy."

Winston squinted. "Who burns what?"

"The rider on Falsetto," Ben said. "Name's Isaac Burns Murphy. From Lexington."

"He any good?" Winston asked, curious now.

"He's young—just eighteen—but he sees things differently out there. We watched him ride last year. Moves like the wind. Don't even need a whip," Ben answered, with admiration in his voice.

Porter scoffed. "Don't care if he rides like a cannonball. No one beats Spendthrift. And that colt's got Edward Feakes!"

Ben stayed steady. "Five cents on it?"

"Easy!" Porter snapped.

They spit in their hands and sealed the bet with a shake.

"Pa, look!" Joshua shouted, tugging his father's arm. "There he is! There's Ike Pa!"

Isaac emerged onto the track, escorted by Eli Jordan and young Edward. He sat astride Falsetto, the chestnut stallion, his posture straight up in the saddle, his colorful silks gleaming in the summer sun.

Isaac leaned down toward Eli. "There's the mustache man."

A few stalls over, riding a hulking bay stallion, was Edward "Mustache" Feakes. His pale skin, green eyes, and heavy mustache gave him a striking, almost regal look.

Eli glanced at the horse. "Yes. And there's the great Spendthrift."

Spendthrift towered over the field—a massive, muscular presence. Falsetto flinched slightly at the sight of him, rearing back.

"It's alright, boy," Isaac murmured, calming the horse. "He's not that much bigger than you."

Then, noticing the size difference up close, Isaac added dryly, "Okay, maybe a little bigger."

Up in the elite section of the grandstand, men in velvet coats and top hats mingled with their finely dressed wives. This was the Gilded Age on full display—ornate bonnets, pearl earrings, fans fluttering, gloves pristine.

Leaning against the balustrade was King Kelly, a debonair White man in his thirties with nimble fingers and charm to spare. He slipped a golden cigar case from the coat pocket of a distracted gentleman, admired it, and then smoothly handed it back to him.

"Forgive me, sir, but I believe this is yours?"

"Good heavens—it is!" the man exclaimed. "Where did you find it?"

"I observed a vagrant trying to make off with it as you entered. I wanted to see it back to its rightful owner."

"You're a fine man!" the gentleman said. "Is there anything I can do to repay you?"

King smiled. "No, no. Courtesy alone."

He paused, then added, "Though... I couldn't help overhear your interest in Spendthrift."

"Indeed," said the gentleman, a carnation pinned to his lapel. "Sterling bloodline. From sire to grand-dam. In sport as in life—it's about breeding."

"Exactly why betting against him would make Midas blush," King said. "Everyone's so confident, no one dares wager the other way. That's why the side pot's so rich."

Carnation leaned in, intrigued. "Is that so? Is there any room left in it?"

"I'm sure we can accommodate a man of your stature," King replied with a sly nod.

Just then, a booming voice interrupted as it strolled through the crowd—"Howdy, my boys!"

It was Lucky Baldwin, a towering White man in his early fifties, all Texas swagger and frontier flair. His white Stetson matched his long silver hair and wild blue eyes.

"I assume y'all wagered your wives on my boy, Silver Star?" Lucky beamed.

Some nodded politely. Others whispered behind gloved hands.

"Who is that?" King Kelly asked.

Carnation whispered back, "That's Lucky Baldwin—California mining baron turned stable owner. A new kind of man for a new age. Money by the fistful—if you can stomach snakes and savages."

Down on the track, the bugler raised his horn and sounded the Call to the Post.

Eli turned to Isaac. "If Falsetto don't jump at the line, you may need to remind him at the corner. Don't wait too long."

Isaac looked down the row at Feakes. "He hasn't even looked at the other horses."

"That's cause he don't think he can lose," Eli replied. "Might not even see you from that high up."

Eli gave Falsetto one last pat. Isaac guided the horse toward the line.

"Here we go, Falsetto. Time to sing," he whispered. "Come on, boy. Remember, we're riding for America."

He patted his mother's Bible in his pocket and the horse's neck and murmured into its ear: "Whatever is true, whatever is honorable and worthy of respect… if anything is excellent or praiseworthy, think about these things—and I will always be with you."

The horses shuffled into position at the starting gate. Isaac steadied Falsetto, measuring the competition. Most of the jockeys were Black, except Feakes, whose pale white skin and curled mustache made him stand out.

Falsetto grew restless, rearing slightly.

"Steady now. Use that feeling, Falsetto. Use it. That's what Uncle Eli says."

BANG!

The starting gun cracked through the air—and they were off.

Falsetto and Isaac were immediately swarmed, falling back to eighth place. Spendthrift surged to a strong lead.

In the grandstand, Ben and Joshua leaned against the rails, eyes wide.

"Spendthrift! My oh my!" Porter shouted with glee.

"Come on, Isaac," Ben whispered.

Isaac waited, eyes scanning the track. No panic. No hesitation. Slowly, methodically, he began to move.

Seventh place. Then sixth. The pace wasn't fast—but it was steady.

Around the first turn, Spendthrift remained far ahead. But Isaac spotted an opening—just a narrow gap between two horses. He leaned forward and guided Falsetto through it with precision. The horse surged.

Then came the outside pass—one, then another. Isaac looked up.

Only one horse remained.

Spendthrift.

Feakes rode the rail, whipping fiercely. The crowd's excited cheers could be heard all the way down on the track. Feakes began waving to the crowd, expecting glory.

But the crowd's cheers weren't for Spendthrift.

They were watching Isaac.

Falsetto soared forward, closing the gap. Isaac spotted an inside lane. He leaned in again. Falsetto responded—thundering forward with such force, that it seemed he rode the wind itself.

Feakes noticed too late. Isaac and Falsetto crossed the finish line—first.

Ben and Joshua leaped into the air. Porter threw his hat to the ground.

In the owners' section, JW Hunt Reynolds, a stiff, proud man in his late thirties, smiled as congratulations rained down.

Nearby, King Kelly noticed Lucky Baldwin, sitting in stunned silence.

"It wasn't the damn horse," Lucky muttered aloud.

His eyes locked on Isaac. That jockey came simply out of nowhere..."

5

America - 1864 - Back at the Tanner Farm

Photograph by Timothy H. O'Sullivan. Courtesy of the Library of Congress, Prints & Photographs Division, Civil War Photograph Collection.

At the dawn of each day, before making beds, it was America's duty to dust the books, and the bookshelves, as well as the large desk in

David Tanner's library. She would run her fingers across the binders, sounding out the book titles under her breath. David's library was her favorite room in the grand house. She had managed to learn to read as a young adult even though reading was not permitted by slaves. Because of her superior skills and good behavior, she had been told by David Tanner to remain quietly seated in a chair in the same room while the Tanner daughters received their reading lessons twice a week. This was only allowed so that America could learn the alphabet to assist her Master in sorting and keeping the books in order by title and subject.

On the tutoring afternoons, as she was seated across the room, she listened intently to the lessons being taught about sounding out words and phrases. She had figured out the rest of the instructions on her own. Writing words was much more difficult for her to learn with no paper or utensils to write with. But she acquired writing skills too, through astute observations. She would use a stick to write words and sentences in the dirt near the slave quarters which she could quickly wipe out if anyone approached.

When a book binding or pages would unravel and the cover of a volume in the Tanner library would wear away or fall off, she was instructed by Master Tanner to throw it out as soon as a new volume could be purchased at the market bookseller. In the dark of night when no one was watching, she would empty the rubbish from the house and retrieve David's discarded books to take back to the slave quarters. The discarded books from Master Tanner's library became America's personal treasures.

She also had a precious small Bible that had been gifted to her by her mother. Her mother had not been able to read it herself, but she told America she acquired it from a kind White Methodist minister working with children in a one-room church building near Lexington.

On this particular morning, America was hard at work in the main house on the Tanner farm. After dusting the library books, she moved with practiced precision to the bedrooms, tucking white bedsheets into the mattresses and smoothing out every wrinkle. Her folded corners were perfect—crisp, tight, symmetrical.

She crossed the room to retrieve a pitcher of water and poured it gently over the pale face of Margaret Tanner, a woman in her forties, seated naked in a bathing basin.

When Margaret was dressed in her undergarments, America stood behind her, combing her hair with care. Margaret gazed into the mirror at her dressing table, her eyes vacant, distant—lost somewhere far beyond the reflection in front of her.

America noticed and spoke in a gentle voice. "That's a fine color on you, Miss Margaret."

"Would you call it honey yellow?" Margaret asked absently.

"I believe it's amber, Miss Margaret."

"Well, it's right beautiful. Especially for the season."

Margaret gave a faint smile, but it disappeared almost as quickly as it appeared.

"The fall came on so sudden this year," she murmured. "I suppose I should be thankful I don't have to wear black. An awful color. No life to it."

"No, a black veil wouldn't suit you, Miss Margaret."

"A small blessing of having three daughters," Margaret said wistfully. "War's such a tiring thing, Meccie. Thank the Lord we live in Kentucky and don't have to choose sides. And thank the Lord my David is too old to enlist. Gray suits his hair better than it would his jacket."

America reached for a brooch on the dresser, but Margaret abruptly caught her wrist.

"No. I've changed my mind," she said sharply. "I'm not ready for fall. Dress me in the lavender sweet."

America nodded calmly, setting the brooch back. "Yes, ma'am."

Later, America tipped a tea kettle into a porcelain cup and placed it carefully on a silver tray. Jenny stood beside her, staring off in a daze.

Once the two of them were alone in the corridor, America leaned in to instruct her.

"When you walk out into the parlor, do it slowly. When you bend to serve, don't jam it under their noses like last time. Hold it just close enough."

"Why?" Jenny asked, sighing. "She didn't say nothin'."

"No. But she thought it," America said quietly.

She waited for a flicker of acknowledgment. Jenny gave a reluctant nod.

"Okay. I'll try to do better next time, America."

"Work to be the best, Jenny. There is no other way."

Jenny picked up the tray and turned to go, but just as she moved toward the parlor, America heard the sound of approaching footsteps. She held out a quiet warning hand to stop Jenny from walking straight into someone's path.

David Tanner passed by, unaware he had nearly collided with the young girl. Jenny looked startled, her chest rising fast.

America whispered firmly, "Listen, Jenny. Always listen. Know your surroundings. Protect yourself, you hear?"

6

America - 1864 - Observation and Intuition

The next day, America and Jenny were back at work. America stood in the corner of the parlor, closely observing as Jenny presented the tea tray—this time more carefully—to Margaret and her visitor, Cynthia.

Cynthia was a White woman in her thirties with tightly pulled-back hair and a sharp, unpleasant expression. Margaret took the cup from Jenny and waved her away with a flick of the wrist. Jenny stepped back and returned to stand beside America, who gave her a subtle nod of approval.

The two White women began to converse loudly enough to be heard across the room.

"The roads aren't so dangerous during the day around Lexington," Cynthia said. "My Jed says he can still trade both ways across the lines without worry. Though he throws in a few extra favors for one side."

"Well, my David says there'll be no danger in these parts," Margaret replied. "Lincoln knows better than to stir up trouble in Kentucky."

Cynthia gave a pointed laugh. "He's wise to leave us alone. If the rest of the South had done the same, they wouldn't be worried about losing their property now."

Margaret turned toward America, "Oh, Meccie?"

"Yes, Miss Margaret," America replied quickly.

"I just received word from Cynthia that the Crawfords won't be coming this week. Their travel plans were spoiled by the weather. We're still expecting the Judsons, though, so we'll need the parlor turned next Thursday."

"Yes, ma'am," America said.

Cynthia coughed politely, then added, "And purchase more apples next market trip, Meccie. The ones you bought are going to rot, I swear."

"I've written you a pass," Margaret said. "Cynthia says the ones we've got aren't worth biting into."

"Yes, ma'am," America replied again, keeping her tone even.

That night, after work had ended, America walked Jenny back to the slave quarters. Dusk was settling over the countryside, the trees were now bare of leaves.

"They don't seem worried much," Jenny said. "Maybe the war ain't comin' as close as folks say."

"No. They're afraid," America said, her tone flat.

"Don't seem afraid to me. How do you know they scared?"

"Miss Margaret lifted her tea by the edges," America observed.

"So?" Jenny asked.

"She usually lifts it by the handle. But if she had, the cup would've rattled and shown her nerves."

"And the apples?" Jenny added.

"They haven't gone to rot. But she's buyin' new ones anyway—for show," America said. "She's tryin' to hold onto control."

Jenny frowned. "But I've seen her tremble. I've seen her cry."

"She's trying to hide her fear, Jenny," America observed. "And those that hide their fear are oft more afraid than those who show it."

7

America - 1864 - Slave Quarter Tension

The eight slaves from the Tanner farm were all congregated around a table in their quarters, eating from a shared platter. Little Isaac sat on America's lap as she helped him carefully spoon the food into his mouth like a gentleman.

Carter, a young and animated field hand in his early twenties, gestured grandly as he finished telling them all a story.

"And Boots Bailey said he learn'd to play a musical in'trament just by dreamin' 'bout it. Said every night he'd lay down and just dream 'bout playin' the fiddle real good. When he woke up in the mornin', he knowed how to play it!"

Sarah shook her head and replied with a grin, "That's Boots for ya. He always got some crazy story. Suppose he dreamed 'bout bein' a rich man, maybe he'd wake up with a pillow full of money."

Carter chimed in with a laugh, "Or dream about a watch so he'd finally show up on time."

"What else you hear, Cart?" Jenny leaned over and asked with curiosity. "What was that you was talkin' about earlier with James?"

"Ah, nothin'," Carter said. "Just that we may be fixin' to get outta here real soon."

Most of the folks gathered around the table stopped eating. They looked up in curiosity and shock.

"Go? How's that?" Jenny inquired again.

"Y'all already know. President Lincoln says we in Kentucky can all be free. All we got to do is run and find a Yankee to take us North," Carter said with confidence.

"Really, Cart? Are you fixin' to leave in a few days?" Sarah asked.

"Yeah, that's what I'm gonna do—leave at the first chance I get. James and me ain't gonna wait much longer. Boots says he can sneak a wagon in for us and—"

"You're wrong," Deacon said, abruptly pushing his chair back from the table.

Carter snapped back, "No, I ain't wrong, man. I heard it from enough hands now. My brother says the same. This ain't gossip, Deek. It's what they call 'mans-pation.'"

"You mean to say the word 'emancipation'?" America replied.

"That's right, Meccie. 'Mancipation," Carter struggled to pronounce the word. "That's it!"

Deacon was not convinced. "That don't apply to us slaves workin' here, Cart."

"Yes, it does! It's the whole United States, Deek, 'specially Kentucky. This is word comin' down from the President himself! A declaration a—"

"No, no... I'm tellin' you— it don't APPLY!" Deacon slammed his hand on the table to make his point.

Carter reeled back. Little Isaac, alarmed by the loud noise and raised voices, started to cry.

The two men continued arguing.

"Kentucky ain't part of no Union and it ain't part of no Confederacy neither," Deacon said knowingly. "We caught up in the middle. That proclamation don't mean nothin' to us. It don't apply." Deacon's voice continued to rise—and so did the tension.

"Deek, please keep it down!" America said as she grabbed Deacon's arm to warn him, then turned to her toddler, Isaac.

"Shhh," she said to Isaac, kissing the top of his head to soothe him.

"Don't worry. There's no trouble here, baby. They just talkin' it out."

Carter searched the faces at the table for some agreement, but none of them reacted positively. They all looked away, avoiding eye contact. Seeing their inaction, Carter's confusion turned into anger.

He looked Deacon directly in the eyes, defiant.

"Just 'cause you're twice my age, you always puttin' me down, Deek. Always tellin' me I don't know nothin'. But I know more than you know. I'm tellin' you—I know."

Deacon held his ground, shaking his head.

"You just talkin' foolishness, Cart. Think 'bout it—what's a piece of paper mean to you anyway? Huh? You really think a piece of paper gonna save you? You'd best get through how we get through. Put your head down and do your work on the farm. Otherwise, your hot-headed ways goin' get you killed—and James too."

Carter stood up abruptly, getting right in Deacon's face, his eyes like daggers.

"That's easy for you to say when you're workin' in the Tanner house, gettin' David Tanner's favor. Those of us in the hot hemp fields don't get to be inside passin' plates around and dustin' counters. Why don't you come out and watch the ones doin' the hard work?"

Sarah interrupted, hoping to defuse the tension.

"Come on now, don't start with that kind of talk, child. You need to be showin' Deacon your respect."

Carter's young spirit could not be contained; his thoughts were running a mile a minute.

"You don't know nothin', Deek. You gonna die out with the times."

The rest of the table tried to resume eating without taking sides.

Isaac cried quietly into his mother's shoulder.

America picked Isaac up and set him on her hip. She walked him to the corner of the room so they could have a private conversation. She lifted his chin and used the hem of her skirt to wipe the tears from his eyes. Then she leaned down and whispered into his ear.

"Just go back to the table and eat your food, Isaac. Don't pay no mind to these men gettin' angry with each other. They care about each other and they're both hopin' for a better life. Someday we're all gonna find a way outta here—to freedom. In the meantime, I'm gonna teach you how to read so your imagination can take you anywhere you want to go."

8

America - 1864 - A Trip to the Marketplace

It was early morning in the slave quarters. America sat beside Sarah, who was sewing while keeping an eye on toddler Isaac, asleep on the floor. America adjusted the blanket around her son as Sarah spoke softly.

"He's got your eyes, but don't cry near as much as you did. Your mama was always holdin' you. She wanted you bad. Skipped out on work, claimin' to be sick. She was sick alright—lovesick."

America gazed down at Isaac. "He looks like a tiny Jerry when he's sleeping."

She smiled faintly. "I just wish I could see Jerry more. I wish he could be here."

"There's a season for everythin', child," Sarah said. "A time to reap, and a time to sew. Right now—we sewin'."

The next morning, America rose before sunrise. It was market day, and she had a list of specific items the Tanners had asked her to buy.

As she made her way down the dirt road, her basket filled with pantry goods, she stopped to inspect a ripe apple. The sound of hoofbeats on cobblestones caught her attention. Looking up, she saw Eli Jordan, a long-time friend of her father's, riding through town on a large black stallion.

Though not yet wealthy, Eli's polished frock coat and freshly shaven face turned heads—even among the White patrons at the market. America set the basket down and rushed toward him.

"Mr. Eli Jordan!" she called.

Eli dismounted, smiling broadly. "America Murphy."

She approached with a grin. "Say, do you train horses or something?"

He laughed. "They mostly train me."

"This one's a beauty," she said, admiring the horse.

"Clancy, they call him. And he is."

"What brings you this way?"

"Just passin' through to Winchester. Gonna purchase a new mare for the Williams & Owings Stables. Stopped in to say hello to a barber. How's your boy?"

"You heard about Isaac?"

"News finds its way."

"Yes. He's already trying to climb over everything."

"Well, if your daddy were still alive, he'd be proud. Probably have him in the saddle already."

America smiled. "I miss him. He'd love to see Isaac now."

"He got me in the saddle myself. I owe Green Murphy for that and so much more. But these days, I'm better off with my feet on the ground."

Before America could reply, a woman came rushing toward them—Cora, a local Black free woman America often saw at the market.

"Meccie, you best come quick!" Cora cried, tugging America's sleeve.

"Hold on, Cora. I'm talkin' to a friend I haven't seen in a while."

"You gotta come now."

Annoyed, America pulled away. "Cora, please..."

"It's Jerry."

Those two words turned everything. America froze. Her breath caught.

Eli saw her face shift. "You best go. I hope everything's alright."

America nodded, then followed Cora urgently around the corner.

Cora pointed through a window.

America hesitated. She didn't want to look—but she had to.

Inside, Jerry stood naked under harsh light. Two White slaveholders circled him like merchants sizing up livestock. His mouth clenched, his eyes shut tight.

America's hand flew to her mouth. She was about to cry out.

Cora quickly grabbed her, pulling her close. "Don't scream. Don't put yourself in danger."

"But Cora…"

"They're sendin' him to Skilling Farm. He's not goin' far. They're sellin' what they got before the war reaches too deep."

"But Isaac is his son. Everyone knows we jumped a broom."

Cora shook her head. "Folks are scared. They're selling what they have before things change."

America watched as Jerry put his clothes back on and was led outside. Prying herself away from Cora, she ran through the alleyway and out into the street to watch, tears streaming down her face. Jerry was being forced onto a wagon by a man with a shotgun along with two other slaves, a young man of twenty years or so and a little boy of no more than eight years. As the cart jolted and drove down the street, Jerry looked back to see his wife standing in the middle of the road.

He stared after her with a yearning but also a numbness, as though his vision of her must be an apparition. As his eyes began to register that she was real…

Cora emerged from the alley and pulled America aggressively away from the street and out of danger. Once the wagon was out of sight, Cora consoled a shocked and troubled America as they walked back through the marketplace and disappeared into the crowd.

Across the street, a group of White and Black folk had gathered around Eli Jordan, admiring his stallion as he mounted up and rode off.

"Must be nice to be a horseman like that," Cora muttered. "Ain't gotta worry about being the one bought and sold."

America stared down the road, watching Eli fade into the distance, still trying to process what had just happened.

9

Isaac - 1879 - Isaac, Up Before the Roosters

It was early morning, and a thick mist hung over the straightaway of the rural racetrack. Isaac was already awake, up before the first hint of sunlight touched the horizon. Inside the stable stall, he sat quietly in the corner, reading a small hard-bound book by lantern light.

After finishing a chapter, he closed the book and put it in his satchel. Then he pulled himself up to a wooden crossbeam and began a set of chin-ups—one, two, five, ten—followed by stretches and sit-ups. Next, he walked over to a nearby rack, where he layered on three heavy coats, one over the other, before heading out for a run.

He sprinted around the track, lap after lap, his breath rising in clouds through the frigid air.

From a distance, Anthony "Tony" Hamilton—a fellow young Black jockey and Isaac's closest friend—watched him from the entrance of the stable. Tony had arrived early, hoping to be the first one there for once, but he found Isaac already mid-run, cloaked in weight.

He waved and gestured that he'd meet him inside.

By the time Isaac returned to the barn, he was sweating profusely beneath the heavy coats. He stripped them off and sat on a bench, wiping the mud from a pair of riding boots with a farrier's hammer. Tony stood nearby, watching.

"I thought I'd be the first one here," Tony said, shaking his head.

"If I could keep at one-fifteen, maybe I'd sleep in," Isaac replied. "But some of us can't be slim-trim Tony Hamilton."

Tony smirked. "Wish that were true. Even back when you were a ninety-pound strapper, you'd still be up before the roosters—readin' books at first light."

He glanced at the coat pile. "What are you at now?"

"Eighteen," Isaac said.

"That's close. Maybe once you clean the mud from your boots you'll be at seventeen. Take those coats off, that's sixteen. A haircut gets you to fifteen. You could use a haircut anyway."

Isaac laughed and flung a clump of mud in Tony's direction. Tony dodged it, grinning.

"You already do your foot lap?" Tony asked.

"Yeah."

"Of course you did," Tony said, grinning again.

"I'd do it again. I'll still beat you."

"No chance."

"Let's see," Isaac said, standing. He jogged back toward the track.

Tony followed, and soon the two stood side by side at the starting line. Stable boys had begun arriving and now gathered along the rails to watch. Among them was the smallest—Lemuel, or "Lemmy," only nine years old.

"Hey Lemmy!" Tony called out. "Give us a start!"

Lemmy pointed at the sky and mimicked the sound of a starting gun with his mouth.

Isaac blinked. "Was that it?"

"Yeah!" Lemmy shouted.

Isaac turned back—only to see Tony already sprinting, ten yards ahead.

Laughing, Isaac took off after him.

By the end of the race, both were winded, bent over at the water bucket outside the stable. They dipped ladles into the cold water, drinking deeply.

"This season's not gonna be the same," Isaac said between breaths.

"Nope. We'll be ridin' the best horses because we've earned it," Tony replied. "And thank God Lemmy won't be soundin' the starting gun."

"And I'll be ahead of you," Isaac said with a wink as he jogged off. "Come on, Tony. Let's go again."

Tony laughed, catching his breath, exhausted. "Not a chance."

10

Isaac - 1879 - The Unpleasant Train Car Ride

The black wheels of the train churned rhythmically as it moved through forest and field. Smoke billowed from the smokestack, curling over treetops as the train passed through both the city and the countryside. It pulled into a bustling station where passengers boarded and made their way to designated cars.

Isaac entered a car filled with upper-class passengers—all of them White. Aware of the eyes already turning toward him, he quietly found an unclaimed seat in a discreet corner.

Nearby, a man in a bowler hat lowered his newspaper and scowled.

"We're trying to have a nice ride here," the man said sharply. "We'd prefer if there wasn't any trouble."

"There's no trouble, sir," Isaac replied calmly.

"You look like trouble," the man said.

"I'm sorry, sir, but I was asked to sit here. I'm waiting for someone."

"Don't try to give me a story. Get back to the other car where you belong."

"Sir, I wouldn't dare give you a story. I'm here at the request of Mr. Hunt Reynolds. He should be here in a moment."

But the bowler hat man was not convinced. "You think you're slick with your smooth talk, hey? Well, whatever your trick is, I don't buy it. Now go and leave us be."

There was an aggressiveness to the man's tone and manner. He was rude and very unkind. A White woman in a bonnet sitting beside him joined in, her piercing eyes fixed on Isaac.

"Just go, please. We'll have a porter fetch you if your master requests it."

"Master?" Isaac said, somewhat defensively.

"Yes," she said, huffing. "You can't just walk anywhere you like on a train car like this."

Just then, Mr. Hunt Reynolds, dressed in his customary three-piece suit, entered the car. He walked directly up to Isaac and the two passengers pressing him.

"Is there a problem here?" he asked.

The bowler-hatted man straightened in surprise. "Is this man someone you know? Is he with you?"

"Yes. This is my jockey."

"Well... he didn't say who he was. Just showed up here in this car."

"My apologies," Hunt Reynolds said. "He'll only be here for a moment."

The man grumbled and returned to his paper. Isaac, feeling the heat rise behind his eyes, turned toward the pair.

"My apologies, sir, and ma'am," he said respectfully.

As Hunt Reynolds began speaking with him, Isaac kept his expression composed, though his hands were clenched at his sides. Outside, the train whistle sounded.

11

Isaac - 1881 - Chester Park Race Day Scuffle

After his first major Stakes win at Saratoga in 1879, Isaac began making a steady living. He earned a modest income and saved every penny. Under Eli's guidance, he joined the local Masonic Lodge, eventually becoming Senior Warden—a rare position of leadership for a young Black man of just twenty years old. Poised, polite, and mature beyond his years, Isaac was becoming the jockey to beat by 1881.

On this particular day, he was set to race at Chester Park in Cincinnati, Ohio. A bugler blew the Call to Post. Isaac rode a sleek, narrow horse named Classmate and took his place near the middle of the line.

On either side of him in the post-stall were two White jockeys—Link and Rose—already at each other's throats.

"They oughta bury you in manure, Link, and steam the fat outta ya," Rose snarled.

"At least I ain't courtin' a girl that looks like your cow," Link snapped.

"You ain't courtin' no one, Link."

"Your girl looks like she got kicked in the face by a horse, but I guess where you come from, that's what a man wants—someone who looks like his mama."

BANG!

The starting signal fired, and the race began.

Link and Rose bolted out in a full sprint, fueled more by spite than strategy. Isaac, composed and calculating, held back. He watched as their feud pushed them too fast, too soon.

By the second furlong, Isaac was gaining. The two rivals were distracted, tiring quickly. Then Rose swerved dangerously, cutting off Link. Link veered back—and raised his whip.

Before anyone could react, Link lashed Rose across the face.

Isaac, boxed in behind them, was caught in the melee. He moved to the outside, trying to avoid the chaos.

Suddenly—

Link leaned over and punched Rose square in the jaw while still riding high in the saddle. Rose rocked back with the force of the blow. His blood sprayed the air and splattered across Isaac's racing shirt. Immediately, Rose careened wildly off the line and was thrown from his horse. The sudden change in direction forced Isaac off-course. He struggled to bring Classmate back in line, but the horse was distracted by the confusion, and was overtaken by the rest of the field.

Ahead, Isaac watched the pack of horses cross the finish line with ease. Frustrated, Isaac finished the race and dismounted his horse. As soon as his boots hit the ground, a racetrack officiant rushed up to him.

"Rider, you're being summoned to the rules committee immediately."

Eli stepped forward from the sidelines, but the official blocked him. "Just the rider."

Isaac waited alone in a quiet corridor. A door ahead bore a brass sign: Executive Committee Office.

After several tense minutes, it opened. A man wordlessly motioned for Isaac to enter.

Inside, the room was paneled in polished wood and lined with silver trophies. Five White men, members of the Chester Park Jockey Club, sat at the end of the room like a tribunal.

Standing before them was John "Admiral" Tinselly—a bearded, agitated former Confederate officer. He addressed Isaac like he was a captured fugitive. "Well, well. What do you have to say for yourself? The Admiral wants to know."

"Respectfully, sir, I don't understand what you mean," Isaac answered.

"Striking another rider is grounds for immediate suspension," Tinselly barked.

"What? I didn't strike anyone, sir."

"You wouldn't even be in this room if it weren't for your owner and his service in the CSA."

Isaac kept his tone even. "With all due respect gentlemen, I don't know what you're talking about."

A panel member leaned forward. "Boy, are you implying that we're stupid—or that you are?"

"Neither, sir. But—"

"Look at your silks," Tinselly snapped in an angry voice. "That your blood?"

Isaac looked down at the crimson splatter. "No. It's not mine. It's Rose's."

"And why is Rose's blood on your shirt?" Tinselly challenged.

"Because Rose and Link were fighting. Rose cut Link off. Link struck him with his whip. Then punched him. I was riding behind them to the outside when it happened. The blood must've flown back."

Tinselly sneered. "Lying will get you nowhere, boy."

"I don't lie," Isaac said calmly.

Tinselly's jaw clenched. Isaac continued, careful but firm.

"We're on the track at furious speeds. If anything—mud, blood, anything—flies, it hits the rider behind, not beside. I don't like to admit I was behind, but I was. I was to the outside."

The room fell silent. Tinselly's lips curled in disgust.

"You're risking more than your reputation, coming in here speaking to us like that."

"You asked me what happened," Isaac replied.

Tinselly, petulant over being contradicted, shook his head in disgust. "Enough!" He barked back at Isaac. "We run a clean sport. We don't tolerate blacklegs, plungers, poisoned horses—or dirty-colored jockeys. Henceforth, you are suspended from all Stakes races."

Isaac stood in stunned silence.

"We'll notify your owner. Now leave."

Isaac paused, then asked, "If I had struck him, wouldn't such a blow direct the blood away from the abuser? If blood were to splatter, would it not splatter on the rider outside and behind the fight when moving at a high rate of speed?"

The panel was again silent.

"You think you're clever?" Tinselly growled. "Careful we don't take away from you more than we already have. You are dismissed and suspended."

12

Isaac - 1881 - Suspended

Stunned, Isaac hurriedly walked through the Chester Park Stables, trying to contain his emotions. Eli, who was seated, waiting on a nearby bench, rose to meet him. "What'd they say?"

Isaac brushed past him. He was determined to set the record straight.

"Where's Link? Where's that devil?" he said with frustration rising in his voice. "Rose must've backed his lie. Threw me under the wagon. I'll make 'em bleed on their own silks—"

"Hey!" Eli snapped. "You'll do no such thing. Get a hold of yourself!"

Isaac ripped off his cap and slammed it to the ground. Eli grabbed his arm and yanked him into an empty stall like a temperamental horse.

"Why'd you go outside? You knew they was fightin'."

"It was my only shot," Isaac replied. "Classmate was losing steam, and I wasn't gonna win boxed in. What—you want me to lose?"

"You can't give 'em a nose, Isaac," Eli said. "You're better than that."

"I am better. That's still not good enough!"

Isaac pulled free from Eli's grasp and stormed off.

"You can't be nothin' if you ain't in the race, son!" Eli called after him.

Inside the locker room, Isaac threw his belongings into a satchel, fuming. Just then, a calm voice broke through the tension.

"Isaac Murphy?"

He turned to see a well-dressed White man with a large gold ring and sharp eyes. It was King Kelly, who first saw him race in New York.

"Yes," Isaac replied, composed but guarded.

"I was told I might find you here. Do you have a moment?"

"I'm sorry, sir, I'm on my way to catch the five-ten train."

"Mind if I walk with you?" King asked.

Isaac sighed. "If you're here to ask me to ride for you, I—"

"No, no, I wouldn't be so bold," King gushed. "I just wanted to meet you. I'm a great admirer. I saw you ride at Saratoga. The way you overtook Spendthrift on the straightaway there… never before have I seen such skill in the saddle. You outthought them. All of them."

"Thank you, sir. But it was Falsetto's day that day." Isaac said, taken back by the high praise.

"Don't be so modest. I know it takes more than a horse. Speed must be guided and pointed in the right direction."

"I appreciate that, sir, but Eli Jordan trained that horse. He deserves the credit. I am just a jockey."

"I didn't see Eli Jordan in the saddle. I saw you," King responded. "Alright then just a jockey, when's your next mount?"

"It's complicated."

"I am quick to learn."

"The short of it is, that I am suspended. They think I was responsible for the brawl on the track today and to blame for another rider's blood on my silks."

"A brawl? On a horse?"

Isaac nodded grimly. "People see what they want. Or say they saw it, even if they didn't."

"What does this mean—for you? And for my sake, what does this mean for those who want to bet on you?"

"It means I am going to have to appeal the suspension," Isaac said with confidence. "And I will win my appeal by telling the truth."

"I'd like to help," the man offered. "Let me see what I can do."

"I can defend myself."

"You should. But even the best men need friends."

Isaac looked at him. "You have to understand, sir, I am not like other riders. I don't play games. I don't trade favors."

"Which is exactly why you should be in this sport," Kelly said, as a train whistle sounded in the distance.

"What's your name?" Isaac asked.

"Most know me as King Kelly. But I answer to either."

King extended his hand, proudly displaying his gold ring. Isaac shook it.

"Thank you, Mr. Kelly."

"We need you, Isaac. We need you on the track where you belong."

Isaac nodded and walked away. King watched him go, his mind calculating their newly formed relationship.

13

Isaac - 1881 - Talk of Snapper

Isaac sat in a dingy train car crowded with other Black passengers. The rhythmic clatter of wheels over the rails echoed around him. He held a copy of *Field & Turf* in his lap, flipping through the pages while deep in thought.

Beside him sat Edward, the stable boy, eagerly scanning a newspaper. The front page featured the headline: SNAPPER WINS AGAIN along with a photograph of the mustachioed popular jockey, Snapper Garrison.

"Snapper keeps winnin'. Maybe it's the mustache," Edward said, nudging Isaac and pointing to the photo.

Isaac chuckled, then glanced at the image.

"Hmm... maybe," he said. "But Edward Feakes had a mustache in '79—less curly, but still—and we beat him at Saratoga."

Edward grinned, folding the paper.

Outside, the landscape passed in a blur of evergreens and open fields. The whooshing rhythm of the train melded with the pulse in Isaac's chest. He stared ahead—totally focused on the future and what he would need to do to compete and win the biggest races in America.

14

America - 1864 - Boots Brings News

At the Tanner Farm, fifteen years earlier, America was at the washboard, her brown arms scrubbing clothes up and down like a piston rod. She paused to wipe the sweat from her brow, then glanced across the autumn fields.

In the distance, a wagon came into view, led by none other than Boots Bailey—the eccentric local fiddler in his fifties Carter and Sarah had talked about, with a crumpled top hat and a glass eye. Boots was well-known among the quarters as an entertainer— delivering stories, songs, and—more importantly—news from beyond the farm.

As he arrived at the slave quarters, Sarah cleared a place at the table for him. America followed shortly behind, curious.

"Hi, Boots," Sarah greeted. "You want soup or somethin' to eat?"

Boots waved her off. "Don't mind me. I live outta my hat."

He pulled off his battered top hat, reached inside, and produced a ripe pear.

"So what's the news today, Boots?" Sarah asked. "More word from the lines?"

"Skies gettin' darker," Boots said, his voice lilting like a tune. "Nights gettin' longer. Wind scratchin' and screechin' like a broken fiddle. Cannons clappin' thunder like the Lord Himself blowin' His nose."

Then he turned to America.

"But I ain't come to spook you—though it's right to be spooked. I came for you, America."

"I told you, Boots, I'm not marrying you," America said playfully.

"Shame," Boots sighed. "That so?"

"That's so. Jerry and I jumped the broom. He's Isaac's father, and we're bound."

"Well then, that's why I'm here," Boots said more seriously. "I heard about Jerry. He enlisted—with his brother Charlie."

"What?" America gasped. "When?"

"'Bout a month ago," Boots replied. "They gone up to Camp Nelson. Lots of colored men enlistin' there. Mostly Northern. But some like Jerry and Charlie found a way out and joined up. If you enlist, they say you're free."

America's face fell. Sarah glanced at her, worried.

"You know what this means, don't you?" Boots said, his tone gentle now. "Some masters and missus come down hard on soldier's wives fightin' with the Yankees. The Tanners may not be the worst, but they could turn mean real fast."

Sarah nodded. "You best listen, Meccie."

Boots leaned in. "The good news is—Camp Nelson's takin' women and children, too. If you're thinkin' of gettin' out... now's the time."

America breathed in deeply, weighing her options. She enjoyed working around the books in Master Tanner's library. She took pride in the way she performed every part of her job on the farm even though it was slave's work. She felt a close bond with Jenny, Sarah, Deacon and the others working around her, even though they were not blood-related. But the love she felt for Jerry was stronger than any love she had ever known.

"I don't stay put long," Boots added. "But I can get you part the way—if you're ready. Has to be day after tomorrow, before first light."

America glanced out the window toward the white farmhouse. Her stomach twisted with both fear and longing. She was not an impulsive person, but in this case, she would have to make a move quickly.

She looked to Sarah, who gave a firm nod.

America turned back to Boots.

"Alright," she said. "First light."

15

America - 1864 -Last Night at the Tanner Farm

The next night, candles flickered in the dining room. Napkins were folded. Forks and knives aligned with quiet precision as America and Jenny prepared the Tanner table for dinner.

Moments later, David and Martha took their seats at opposite ends with their daughters seated in the middle.

As the meal progressed, America noticed how graceful Jenny had become. Her movements were efficient and quiet. The tray didn't rattle anymore. She filled glasses before they were empty. She anticipated every need before it was voiced.

Jenny had learned well. And the dinner passed in complete silence.

16

America - 1864 - America Says Goodbye

Later that evening, America sat on the floor beside Jenny, holding her hands tightly.

"And when she asks, you say…?" America coached.

"She caught a terrible sickness in the night. America and her boy," Jenny recited.

"That'll buy us some time," America said. "You do everything perfect like we practiced. They will get used to us bein' gone and won't miss a thing. Dig a grave for us. Then fill it in. Say we ran wild with the fever and was likely to die someplace else—or make everyone in the Tanner house dreadful sick."

America pulled a soft, boxy pillowcase into her lap and handed it to Jenny.

"What's this?" Jenny asked, her voice trembling.

Inside were two tattered books with frayed spines and worn-off covers.

"Keep reading," America said. "Remember what I've been teaching you. Keep tryin'. Once you know how, it's yours forever. No one can ever take that away from you. Understand?"

"What if I don't know a word yet?"

"Sound it out like we practiced. Then write it out with a stick in the dirt. The story'll give you a clue. Reading's a puzzle—and you can solve it."

Jenny traced the spine of one book. "The Count of… Montee Crist-oh?"

"Cristo," America corrected. "Monte Cristo."

"What's it about?"

"Revenge. Love. Patience," America answered. Then softly: "All human wisdom is in two words—wait and hope."

Jenny clutched the book to her chest, tears falling freely now. She curled into America's arms.

"I'm scared," she whispered.

"Don't be," America said, stroking her hair. "We'll see each other again. I promise."

She looked across the quarters at those who had become family: James. Carter. Deacon. Sarah—who was holding little Isaac in her arms.

This was her home. These were her people.

But she knew she had to go.

For Isaac. For Jerry. For the life waiting beyond the fields.

17

America - 1864 - First Light

Sarah kept careful watch, her eyes fixed on the darkened path beyond the quarters. When she saw the faint silhouette of Boots' wagon approaching, she turned and gave a silent signal to America.

Without a word, America wrapped the sleeping Isaac in a shawl, lifted him gently into her arms, and carried him out. She climbed into the back of the cart as quietly as she could. Boots, already seated and ready, nodded once.

The horse obeyed the reins, and the wagon creaked to life, rolling out onto the dirt road with a slow, deliberate rhythm.

America didn't speak. She simply held her son close. As the wagon moved further into the woods, the sky behind them began to glow—a faint shimmer of dawn just peeking over the trees. Clouds gathered at the horizon like messengers of a long-awaited change.

This was the beginning of a new chapter. Her hands trembled slightly, not from fear but anticipation. She was on her way to Jerry to reunite him with his wife and son before he would head into a battle for their freedom. And for the first time in her life, she was headed toward what she hoped would be a brighter future.

18

America - 1864 - Morning on the Outskirts

Golden light filtered through the trees as the wagon rattled along a rutted path. The sun had just broken the horizon when Boots brought the horse to a sudden stop near a clearing at a crossroads.

He pointed ahead through a tangle of brush. "It's not much further now," he said. "I'd take you the rest of the way, but I don't want 'em shootin' at me."

America's eyes widened. "Oh my God. They're not going to shoot at us, are they, Boots?"

"I hope not," he replied with a half chuckle. "They're a lot less likely to shoot at a woman and child than at an old man with a fiddle. But best move quick all the same."

He flicked the reins, and the horse stirred restlessly.

America glanced back at him, then looked ahead toward the woods beyond the clearing. The way forward was silent, ominous.

She took a breath, lifted Isaac into her arms, and stepped off the wagon.

Without turning around, she gathered her skirt and took her first determined step toward freedom.

19

America - 1864 - Milly and Louisa

America emerged from the woods into an open field where a fortified Union depot stood in the distance. Its perimeter was lined with an interlocking snake fence and watchtowers. Beyond it, rows of tents stretched out like stitched fabric across the horizon.

She followed the fence line until she spotted a crowd—dozens of women and children gathered in a long, weary line outside the depot's main gates. Some stood. Others sat. Many huddled together against the cold.

She joined the end of the line and settled next to a young teenage girl who held an infant swaddled tight to her chest.

The girl glanced over and offered a warm, tired smile.

"Didn't think the line would be this long," America said.

"Me neither," the girl replied. "We've been here since sundown yesterday. Hid out near Wilmore for a few nights before that. Word is more folks are comin' behind us."

She adjusted her shawl. "My name's Milly. You ain't got no blanket?"

"No," America admitted. "Foolish of me. We left in a rush."

Milly reached into her satchel and handed her a spare. "Here. Got an extra."

"Bless you," America said with genuine relief. She turned to her son. "What do we say, Isaac?"

"Thank you very much, ma'am," he said shyly.

Milly beamed. "You're very welcome, Isaac. You're a little gentleman."

Then she turned to America. "What's your name?"

"America. And yours?"

"Milly. This here's Louisa," she said, gently pulling back the folds of cloth to reveal a tiny, sleeping baby girl.

Hours passed slowly. The sun climbed higher in the sky. Finally, a slender White soldier emerged from the gate, looking half-awake, his uniform rumpled. His badge read Private Combs.

He glanced over the crowd and motioned Milly forward with her baby. Then he waved America and Isaac to follow.

"How many?" Combs asked.

"Just my son and me," America replied.

"Your husband enlisted here?"

"Yes, sir. Jerry Burns. He came with his brother, Charlie. Just over a month ago."

Another officer thumbed through the enlistment logs behind him.

"Where are you coming from?" Combs asked.

"From a small farm, sir," she said.

Combs gave a wry smirk. "You know what I mean."

America straightened her shoulders. "I'm coming from a place I don't want to go back to. I came to be with my husband. The boy's father."

Combs studied her for a long moment. "Outside Lexington, huh?"

"Yes, sir."

He leaned forward slightly, lips curled into something between a smirk and a sneer. "Well, alright."

She tried to remain composed. "I can cook. Clean. I work hard."

Combs looked down to see Isaac trying to climb the snake fence beside the entrance.

"Isaac!" America called. She rushed forward and scooped him into her arms. "He's three, almost four. Thinks he's a soldier."

Combs looked at the boy, then at her again. With a grunt, he relented.

"Fine. Find a tent in the outer field. Any tent not taken. You're logged."

He turned to the officer beside him. "One woman, one child. Mark it."

20

America - 1864 - Camp Nelson Refugees

America found a small patch of space inside a narrow tent and began to unpack the few belongings they had.

"Mama, how long we here for?" Isaac asked, gazing up at her with wide eyes.

"Not long if you keep climbing on things," she said, giving him a firm look. "No climbing."

"Not even on the bed to sleep, Mama?" he asked, voice innocent and pleading.

"Oh, you think you're clever, huh?" she replied, turning to face him with a raised brow.

Isaac giggled.

"Now listen to me," America said as she crouched to his level. "There's lots of soldiers around here. A good soldier stands tall and straight. No slouching. No trouble. A good soldier listens to his mama. Understood?"

Isaac saluted.

"That's my proud soldier. A proud, courageous soldier, just like your daddy."

21

America - 1864 - Isaac Meets His Father

Outside the tent, America stood still, scanning the rows of tents. In the distance, a group of Black Union soldiers approached, some peeling off as they spotted their families. Then her eyes lit up.

Jerry, clad in Union blue, came running toward her. Beside him was his lanky younger brother, Charlie Burns.

"Jerry! My Jerry!" she cried, throwing her arms around him, knocking his cap off in the process. He didn't seem to mind.

They clung to each other. Then America turned to Charlie, who stood smirking.

"You happy to see me too?" he teased.

"Charlie? Or should I say, Officer Charles?" America laughed. "Still skinnier than a broomstick."

They hugged.

As Jerry bent to retrieve his cap, America spotted Isaac, standing shyly just inside the tent flap.

"Come on, Isaac—it's your father," she coaxed.

Isaac walked over slowly, his shoulders slouched, clearly overwhelmed.

"Son," America said gently, "what did we just say about slouching?"

She turned to Jerry, smiling. "He wouldn't stop talking about you. Says he wants to be a strong soldier like his daddy."

"He's got that fighting spirit," Jerry said proudly. "You're a brave boy, Isaac. Aren't you?"

Isaac nodded.

"It's been a while, huh?" Jerry added. "You've grown stronger. Maybe even as strong as me."

"I'm not that strong," Isaac murmured.

"No, you are," Jerry said, kneeling. "You could probably lift me up. Go on—try!"

Isaac wrapped his arms around Jerry's legs and strained. Jerry rose up on his toes, pretending to be lifted.

"Whoa!" he said in mock surprise. "You are strong!"

Isaac laughed in amazement. "Now me! Try me!"

Jerry crouched, and made exaggerated grunts and groans. "Oooh... can't do it! You're too heavy!"

"Try harder!" Isaac demanded.

America watched the playful exchange with joy in her eyes.

"That the best you got?" she teased.

Finally, Jerry hoisted Isaac into the air.

"See! I knew you were stronger than me!" Isaac cheered.

"Only for now," Jerry said, holding his son close. "You're going to get there someday."

He knelt again and placed a hand on Isaac's small shoulder. "I'm glad I got to see you and your mama before I head out tomorrow."

America's face fell. "Tomorrow? When are you coming back?"

"When we finish whupping 'em, I reckon."

"But... Boots Bailey said y'all enlisted only a month ago?"

"Five. Five months ago, Meccie," Jerry said quietly.

The joy drained from her face.

"It's not Boots' fault," Jerry added gently. "We had to be careful who heard. I'm just glad Boots got word to you. He's one of the few who could've helped you get here. Then again, you probably would've found your way blindfolded."

He lifted her chin.

"How about some food? I brought your favorite."

He pulled a tin can from his satchel and gave it a shake.

"Lookie here… beans!"

Jerry opened the tent flap, and they stepped inside. Charlie knelt and looked Isaac in the eye.

"Isaac? You've got a job to do now. You have to protect your mama while we're gone. Can you promise me that?"

For a child so young, the words appeared to register with him. Isaac studied his uncle's face seriously, then nodded.

Charlie smiled, tousled his nephew's hair, and led him into the tent to join his mother and father.

22

America - 1864 - Onward to Battle

The sound of a Black fife player echoed across the field, playing The Battle Hymn of the Republic. A large regiment of Black Union soldiers marched out of Camp Nelson with solemn determination.

Lining the road were families—women and children—cheering them on.

America stood among them, holding Isaac high so he could see above the crowd. His eyes scanned the line of soldiers until he spotted Jerry and Uncle Charlie among them, marching proudly.

Isaac's small hand waved. Jerry raised a hand back and smiled broadly.

23

America - 1864 - Back in the Barracks

Life at Camp Nelson settled into a routine. America, along with a dozen women and girls, cleaned the barracks each day—sweeping floors, scrubbing surfaces, and emptying bedpans.

America worked with quiet resolve. One afternoon, while sweeping in a corner, she noticed a girl no older than nine or ten, standing uncertainly.

"Little one," America said kindly. "You know how to sweep?"

The girl nodded.

America handed her the broom. "Stay busy. Stay safe."

At mealtime, America and Isaac waited in line for the camp's thin gruel—barely better than what slaves had received on the Tanner farm. The portions were meager, just enough to keep moving.

Days passed, all much the same.

Each afternoon, America read to Isaac from the small Bible she had brought that had once belonged to her mother. Together, they sounded out stories—Noah, Jonah and the Whale, Joseph's Coat, the Sermon on the Mount. At night, she read from a small, frayed book of Shakespearean sonnets as he drifted off to sleep.

More days passed. Still no word of when the men might return.

America cared for Isaac—and for Milly, who nursed Louisa while Isaac played in the dirt nearby. From sunup to sundown, America worked: sweeping, carrying water, washing clothes, making sure every surface was clean.

At night, she curled up beside Isaac, hoping for rest. But every night, a woman near her tried to soothe a sobbing girl, and sleep never came easy.

Days turned into weeks.

The number of women in the barracks tripled. Many stood idle, unsure how to help. Others sat, exhausted from their journeys.

One morning, as America carried out a bedpan, she overheard voices nearby.

She paused behind the corner of the building as Private Combs argued with a middle-aged, barrel-chested officer.

"That's not what I'm saying at all," the Captain snapped.

"I'm just saying—there's too many of them. It's become an infestation."

America slid closer, straining to hear.

"What are we gonna do—turn them out into the woods?" Combs asked, concerned.

"Yes," the Captain answered coldly. "That's exactly what we're going to do. This ain't a hotel, Combs. We're in the middle of a war."

"But, sir, some of them work hard. They clean the barracks—"

"Spare me. They've had a warm place, food, shelter. It's more than most. Their husbands are gone—and most ain't coming back."

Combs hesitated.

"They can go back to where they came from," the Captain added sharply.

"And if they don't have anywhere to go?" Combs pressed.

"Then they'll figure it out. But this comes from General Fry, not me. It's final and it's damned freezing out here. So handle it, Combs. Now. Dismissed."

The Captain turned and began walking toward the barracks.

America peeled away, slipping back into the shadows before she could be seen.

24

America - 1864 - Cast into the Woods

America entered the barracks with her empty bedpan, taking in the sight of over fifty women and children, each trying to look busy and useful.

"Attention!" Private Combs barked through a megaphone, flanked by two officers America didn't recognize. They marched through the tent village, now a chaotic sprawl of makeshift shelters.

Hundreds of refugees stood shivering in the bitter cold.

"General Fry has ordered that all non-military personnel gather their belongings and vacate the grounds of Fort Nelson immediately," Combs declared. "If you do not leave by sundown, all belongings will be seized, and you will be forcibly expelled."

Cries of panic rippled through the crowd. A young girl gasped.

"For your own good, I am ordering you to leave immediately. This decision is final," Combs added before snapping his heels and marching off.

Back in the tent, America sat beside Milly, who rocked baby Louisa and hummed a lullaby between coughs. The cold was brutal—Milly's face looked touched by frostbite.

"Maybe they're just saying this to scare us off," Milly said weakly. "That's what happened last time."

"No, Milly," America said. "This time is different."

"But it was the same speech?"

"Same words. But last time, Combs lingered. He almost apologized. This time, he couldn't look us in the eye."

"They mean to put us out... or let us die," she said flatly.

Milly looked terrified. "But they can't do this. Don't they care what happens to us?"

"I wouldn't bet on it."

Within the hour, America heard shouting and the sound of wood splintering. She peeked through the tent flap—soldiers were smashing shelters with hammers and axes.

In the distance, Captain Smith raised his voice. "Light them up!"

Torches ignited a heap of tents and timber soaked in oil. The flames exploded skyward.

America gripped Isaac's hand as soldiers began shoving women toward the snake fence.

"Out!" they shouted, spitting at the terrified families.

"Where? I—I don't know where to go!" one woman cried.

"OUT! MOVE!" a soldier yelled, pointing directly at America and Isaac.

Behind him, America watched in horror as women and children were struck with rifle butts.

She scooped Isaac into her arms and began running. As night fell, they stumbled through the icy dark toward the forest. At the tree line, America turned and saw the camp behind them engulfed in flames, its orange glow turning the sky into a roaring furnace.

25

America - 1864 - Freezing in the Forest

Hours passed. Along with hundreds of others, America moved through the cold, dark woods, carrying Isaac. No one seemed to know where they were going.

Exhausted and numb, the women staggered forward. America noticed a large group veering off the path.

"Where are they going?" she asked.

Betsy, a middle-aged woman nearby, answered while trying to soothe a weeping teenage girl.

"They say they saw a mule shed up yonder. That's where they're headed."

"You're not going with them?"

"Nope. I'm followin' Rose Anne. She says there's an old Indian cabin near the river."

"Says?" America raised an eyebrow. "Is everyone just guessing now?"

She looked down. Isaac was shivering beneath his thin blanket. America took the one off her back and wrapped it around him.

Suddenly, her eyes widened. "Milly. Milly and the baby—have you seen them?"

She scanned the scattered figures.

"Milly?" she called. "Are you back there?"

Betsy shook her head. "I don't think she's with us. Might've gone the other way."

Panic gripped America at the thought of losing sight of young Milly and her baby, Louisa, realizing they were already suffering from sickness.

"Isaac come with me," she said sternly, turning around. "I'm going back to find them." America's heart was pounding deep in her chest, imagining the worst.

"Meccie, you can't!" Betsy called out. "You'll freeze!"

But America was already stumbling through the trees, Isaac in tow.

"Milly!" she called to every group she passed, jogging up to scattered groups of women and children.

She wandered further into the wilderness until ahead of her in a clearing, she observed a body on the ground near a fallen tree.

"Stay here," she instructed Isaac. "Don't move. You just keep looking that way and watch where they're going."

America ran over to the body. She bent down and pulled back the shawl to see closed eyes and frozen skin. Tears filled America's eyes and began pouring down her brown, cold cheeks. "Milly, baby, Louisa.…Milly.…" America whispered their names softly with desperation in her voice.

America shook her friend by the shoulders. There was no response. She palmed Milly's face, ice cold to the touch. Far ahead, a concerned Betsy continued to call out through the darkness. Betsy had followed America and Isaac back partway and was still in earshot.

"Meccie!" Betsy's voice rang out. "They're gone, baby. They was both real sick. Don't get lost now too! You and Isaac got to keep your blood movin'!"

America's hands shook as she unwrapped the bundle that Milly was holding. She pulled back the folds and began to sob uncontrollably.

Through the freezing night she heard Betsy calling out again "Meccie! We all need you! I am begging you! Move on and live!" Betsy pleaded.

America looked over and saw Isaac standing obediently where he had been told to remain, shivering but still very much alive.

"Mama, I'm cold," he called softly. "Please, Mama. Let's go back to Betsy. I'm scared."

America looked at the lifeless baby in Milly's arms and then back to her own shivering son. She pulled her Bible from her pocket, and whispered a prayer over Milly and Louisa before she began walking back to her son. She took Isaac's hand without speaking a word and stumbled her way back in the cold, dark night to Betsy and the group of women remaining, determined to fight for their survival.

At last, after what felt like endless hours, a small snow-covered structure appeared through the trees.

Betsy had been right.

Inside the dilapidated cabin, the women huddled on the dirt floor. America knelt by the fireplace, clearing away snow and soot.

"Anyone have a match?" she asked.

No answer.

"Flint? A match?" she asked again, desperate.

Finally, a trembling hand extended a small box.

"Bless you," America whispered. "We made it."

She lit a match and stoked a small flame, coaxing warmth into the space.

"We need kindling—sticks, twigs, anything dry. If you're not moving, huddle close." Two women returned with the needed kindling and soon a blaze of heat filled the room.

As America tended the growing fire, Betsy sat beside her.

"I think we're near the old boarding house," she said. "The folks there—good folks—they might help us. But we won't last here long."

"You should rest," Betsy added gently.

"Not until the others are safe," America replied. "Thank you for caring about us, Betsy. God will bless you for encouraging Isaac and me to keep going, when all seemed lost. My heart is broken for Milly and Louisa."

"It was for selfish reasons, America," Betsy said as she put her arm around her. "You are irreplaceable, and the hardest worker I have ever known."

Later that night, America stroked Isaac's hair and said a prayer of thanksgiving that he was sleeping peacefully beside her. She kept the fire burning until she was sure everyone in the room was fast asleep.

26

Isaac - 1881 - Isaac Meets Lucy at Craw Bottom

Though still suspended from racing, Isaac had made a compelling case for reinstatement. While he awaited a decision, he kept close to his best friend Anthony Hamilton, attending races and staying connected to the sport he loved.

One evening, Isaac found himself at Craw Bottom, a lively pub and dance hall in a Black community just outside of Frankfort, Kentucky.

A fiddler played a jig, a bass thumped rhythmically, and a washboard rasped in tempo. The room bustled with joy and music.

At a corner table, Isaac sat with Anthony and a few others. He wasn't speaking much and he had a sad look on his face.

"You alright, Ike?" Tony asked. Isaac nodded but looked distant.

"Don't beat yourself up," Tony continued. "You're gonna win that case and get back in the saddle. You'll be alright. They can't keep you down for long. They won't admit it, but they miss seeing you on the track."

"I feel like I'm running races in my head, Tony. Over and over. Every track, every horse. I can't stop thinking about it."

"The suspension's a gift if you let it be. Time to breathe, to reset. There's a silver lining if you look for it."

Isaac's gaze drifted across the room.

A young light-skinned Black woman in a cream-colored dress had caught his eye. She moved with grace, her presence luminous.

Her name was Lucy Carr, though Isaac didn't know it yet.

"She's something," Tony said, following his friend's gaze.

"Maybe you're right," Isaac replied to Tony as he continued to admire the lovely sight in front of him.

As the young woman of sixteen years moved gracefully, Isaac was caught up in Lucy's beauty and class. He couldn't take his eyes off of her. He finally decided to get up the nerve, rising from his seat to approach Lucy.

From the table, the rest of the men watched as Isaac easily began to converse with her. Before long, Isaac was extending a hand and Lucy was accepting his invitation to dance. They begin whirling across the dance floor.

They danced—swooping, stomping, whirling to the rhythm of the fiddle. Isaac's steps, learned from his mother, were spirited and precise. They performed traditional jigs, never touching one another but rounding and passing each other in a series of dips. Their dance steps were joyful.

During a particularly energetic move—SNAP. Lucy's heel gave way, and she tumbled into Isaac's arms.

A flash of concern crossed Isaac's face until Lucy looked up at him and began laughing uncontrollably. Isaac helped her to a bench.

"This has never happened to me before," she said. "I'm usually sure on my feet. I blame the shoes."

Isaac knelt, examining the heel. "Don't worry. I work with shoes all the time. Horseshoes, mostly."

Lucy burst into laughter again. "Am I a horse now?"

"That bad?" Isaac grinned. "I beg your pardon, Miss, but I happen to like horses quite a bit. As a matter of fact, I love them."

"I hope you're not planning to nail anything onto me."

Isaac made a mock-serious face. "I wouldn't dream of it."

As he tried to fix the shoe, the heel popped off again.

"Maybe I should tack it like a horse," he joked.

Lucy shuddered. "How do horses stand it?"

"They don't feel it," Isaac said, his voice softening. "It's like our fingernails—only the edges feel nothing. But right in the middle, where it's soft... that's where you have to be careful. That's where they feel everything."

He looked up, handing the shoe back to her.

"Here you are, Miss."

"Lucy," she said, smiling. "My name's Lucy."

That night marked the beginning of something beautiful. From that day forward, Lucy and Isaac, both avid readers, began meeting at the Lexington Community Library. They walked for hours, discussing books, life, and dreams.

Shortly after he met Lucy Carr, Isaac's suspension was lifted. He was once again eligible to ride in Stakes races.

With love in his heart and purpose in his stride, his life was turning.

Two years later, on January 24, 1883, Isaac Burns Murphy married Lucy Carr at St. John's African Methodist Church in North Frankfort, Kentucky.

A description of their wedding appeared in the local Lexington newspaper. In it, the column described Lucy's wedding dress and jewelry: "Lucy Carr Murphy wore white silk trimmed with pearls and white lace, and ornaments of diamonds and gold."

27

Isaac - 1883 - Nuptials and Honeymoon Train

Flower petals cascaded over Isaac and Lucy as they stepped out of the chapel, newly married. The scene overflowed with well-wishers—both White and Black—admiring and celebrating the handsome couple. Heading off on their honeymoon, Isaac and Lucy sat together in a fancy train car, undisturbed. Other patrons, all White, were seated in various other compartments. Isaac and Lucy held hands and admired the passing scenery through the train window, basking in the joy of their new marriage.

A well-dressed White man with a large top hat entered the car. He wore a three-piece suit and fine shoes, his eyes darting around as if searching for someone. When his gaze landed on the couple, he lit up with excitement.

"Excuse me? Are you Isaac Burns Murphy?"

"Yes, sir, I am. And this is my wife, Lucy. We were just married and are on our way to celebrate our honeymoon," Isaac responded politely.

"Oh my God, I can't believe it," the man said, barely able to contain himself. "I hope I'm not being presumptuous, but may I shake your hand and get your autograph? I've never met a celebrity before. I saw you race at Saratoga in '79 and again earlier this year at Latonia. You're the greatest horseman I've ever seen ride a Thoroughbred."

"Of course, sir, I'd be honored," Isaac said.

The man gave Isaac a firm handshake and handed over a notepad and pen. Isaac signed it and returned it to him. The man left grinning from ear to ear, and the newlyweds breathed a quiet sigh of relief.

28

America - 1865 - Refugee Rescue

Photo Credit: Keeneland Library Hemment
Collection

The sound of hoofbeats came to a stop. America's eyes flashed open. The door to a decrepit boarding house swung open, letting in a gust of wind and snow. In stepped Eli Jordan, carrying baskets of food in both hands.

A mousy-looking Black woman in tattered clothes lifted her head from the check-in desk.

"I'm here to help," Eli said urgently. "I heard there were refugee women and children from Camp Nelson here?"

"Yeah, some of 'em are here alright," the woman said through a hacking cough. "I'll take you back."

Eli covered his mouth with a scarf and stepped through a broken doorway into the makeshift sleeping quarters. Row upon row of cots were filled with tired, sick women and children.

Without a word, Eli began handing out food from his satchels. Women and children reached out desperately for what he had. Then he noticed one cot that hadn't stirred.

He approached cautiously and froze when he recognized the emaciated face of America.

"Oh dear Lord—Mr. Eli Jordan," she whispered, smiling faintly through cracked lips.

"America, is that you? Are you sick? Let me see your hands. Where's your son?"

She held out her hands, almost purple from the cold. She pulled back the blanket to reveal Isaac, curled beside her, thin and asleep.

Shock and anger filled Eli.

"How could the Union Army let this happen—after all our men have given?" he muttered. "Come on. You and the boy are coming with me."

America weakly protested, "We don't want to be a burden..."

"I know you're proud, but I owe your father a debt I intend to repay."

Eli helped her up. He extended the baskets he was carrying that were now empty of bread to transport her belongings in. "Where are your things? Come on now, get your things."

America reached under the cot to locate her mother's Bible and a bag of small books she had carried with her through the journey and Milly's blanket as if they were priceless treasures. "Come on now, get your clothes and other things," Eli said again after taking the book bag in hand. America shook her head. It was clear that there were no other belongings to get.

"That's alright. Let's go," Eli said as he helped America stand and scooped up little Isaac in his arms. The three of them quietly exited the boardinghouse. Eli helped America and Isaac into the carriage he had parked outside with a stagecoach driver waiting with the horse hitched to a fence post. He untied the reigns from the post, and jumped into the carriage before they all drove off into the dark night.

29

America - 1865 - Warm Welcome at the Jordans

A stagecoach arrived at a stately two-story home. Eli told the driver to wait with America and Isaac while he went inside to tell his wife what had happened.

A few moments later, Eli returned, opening up the coach door to help America and Isaac out.

"Go on in and meet my wife, Lily, and my girls, Emily and Lydia."

Lily Jordan, a graceful woman in her late forties, rushed to greet them.

"Come to me now, let's get you warm and fed. Poor thing is rail thin, Eli."

Eli turned to his wife. "I'll be back after returning the coach."

Inside, Lily and her daughters served biscuits, sausage, beans, and turnips. Isaac devoured his meal, America could manage only a few bites.

"I hate to trouble you," America said, "but thank you for your wonderful hospitality."

"No trouble at all," Lily replied. "You eat, and then I'll pour a warm bath and make you up a bed to sleep away that fever."

While they were finishing up, Lily proceeded upstairs and poured a bath for America. Once the water was drawn, she walked her up slowly. She helped America remove her ragged clothes and placed her in the warm water. While America was bathing, Lily went back downstairs and instructed her two daughters to make up bedding for Isaac and keep him comfortable on the couch in the front room.

Lily helped America towel off and put on a clean nightgown before walking her over slowly to the bed and pulling a set of covers over her shivering body to put her to sleep. She whispered in her ear,

"We're going to take care of you and Isaac, America. Eli has told me that your father, Green Murphy, was a fine man and we will make sure his family is provided for until they can make it on their own in good health."

"I am so grateful to you, Miss Lily," America said weakly. "Eli saved our lives tonight and has given me hope. But I do not intend to be a burden to you. We will get on as soon as we can and pay you in time for your kindness."

"That won't be necessary, Meccie, just feel better and sleep well tonight," Lily said softly as she moved to leave the room. America stopped her, "But Lily, I need to care for my Isaac...where is he now?" She began to move from the bed, trying to get up.

Lily pushed her gently back down, "Don't you worry. Emily and Lydia are tending to him. They will tell him a bedtime story and put him to sleep on the couch downstairs. You just stay under these blankets and warm yourself up. Shhh. You've got to rest. You call if you need anything, okay?"

Lily removed the lantern from the bedside table and walked to the door where Eli was now standing looking in at America with a face that read of worry and guilt. The two of them closed the door, leaving America behind in the moon-glow darkness.

America turned over and looked at the floor, witnessing the flecks of snow shadows falling slowly across her. She began to drift in and out of sleep. In her dream state, she saw something in the corner of the room. It was Milly, young and warm, holding her baby and speaking to her, "It's okay America, we're alright now."

America shivered, deeply afraid of the fever dream that had suddenly appeared before her. She sat up and turned to look out of the window. As she did, she believed that she clearly saw Milly waving up at her.

"You'll be alright, Meccie," she heard Milly say. The vision continued as she saw young Milly turn and walk across the snowy fields, holding her baby Louisa until she disappeared into the darkness.

America's gaze lingered on the yard. As she squinted to see clearly, she realized that she was looking at a large tree that had thin lines of white snow covering its branches.

30

America - 1865 - Time Passes at the Jordans

Over the next several months, America became stronger. As she regained strength, she observed the same tree she noticed in the yard on her first night in her fever dream change. First, it was covered with snowfall, then it was drenched with heavy rain. Finally, more weeks passed and sunlight shown down on the tree and new buds started to form on its boughs. Underneath its branches, out the same window, America observed Eli leading a small, beautiful horse, encouraging it in a gentle voice into a yard filled with springtime air and green grass.

America, now in full health, looked out of the window as Eli Jordan could be seen smoothing out the mane of a beautiful grown horse.

31

America - 1865 - A New Day in the USA

Eli entered his home after a long day at the stables. He took off his gloves, hung his hat on a hook, and looked over his house. The floors, lamps, bureaus, and every corner of every room was impeccably clean. He smiled, knowing who had done such great work.

Hours later, Eli, America, Lily, Isaac and the two Jordan girls now, eleven and thirteen, were sitting at the kitchen table eating dinner, conversing.

"You know that it's no trouble for us having you here, Meccie," Eli spoke up. This house shines like a new penny since you've been working it. You can stay as long as you like."

Lily smiled in agreement, "I agree with Eli, and our girls adore Isaac."

"I know your boy loves reading," Eli continued, "but I believe I can get him a job as a stable boy soon. He's the right size and if he's got any of his grandfather Green Murphy in him, he'd be a great rider too."

"That's kind of you to offer to help us, Eli," America responded. "But I really want Isaac to go to school to get better educated. Maybe he could be a teacher or a lawyer or a businessman one day." There was a pause and then she went on to say, "Riding is dangerous. We have had our fill of danger."

Eli raised his eyebrows, "Riding is 'bout as dangerous as anything else in this life."

"True, but when Daddy was thrown, he never walked right again and he struggled to talk, Eli," America recalled.

"I understand," Eli said with compassion. "What happened to Green was hard, but becoming a horseman is one of the few things we can do with pride. There are risks, but it gives a man of color a better life if he's smart. And it also teaches him other important lessons that you can't learn in a classroom. Your father knew that."

"Either way, it's time that we get along. You and your whole family have been more than generous with us. And we thank you for everything you have done for us," America said.

Eli spoke to Lily as he referred back to America. "Headstrong this one, isn't she?"

Then he turned back to America, "Truth is, Meccie, I believe that Isaac has talent and brains and courage like you and his father and grandfather. And I will teach him to ride as safe as I can. He would make an excellent jockey someday. I want to train him to be a success."

Outside, at that moment, there came an unexpected loud hooping and hollering. Eli, confused and concerned, stood up and began heading towards the door. Once there, he opened it and inquired with a young man standing in a group nearby on the street, "What's the meaning of all this noise?" Eli asked.

"It's over. Lee surrendered to the good General Grant. They did it. Those boys did it!" the young man said.

There was a knowing silence in the Jordan household for a moment. Then the news sank in.

"Oh My God! America! Hallelujah!" Lily exclaimed, coming out the door with her girls close behind.

"They did it. You hear that Emily, Lydia, Isaac?!. They did it!" Eli shouted with joy. All three children cheered. One of the girls lifted Isaac high into the air.

Lily was almost breathless. "They're coming home, Meccie, Jerry will be coming home!"

"Jerry! Oh my Jerry!" America exclaimed. "Isaac, your daddy will be coming home!"

32

America - 1865 - Fort Nelson News

America held a bonnet to her head on a blustery day as she hurried down the steps to an awaiting wagon. The Jordan's valet helped her climb on board. She had a very bumpy ride in the coach to Fort Nelson but she was so filled with excitement that all she could think about was Jerry.

The wagon pulled up in front of Camp Nelson and America stepped out. She made her way through the Union Depot, a depot much different from the one she left behind when she and Isaac were expelled, along with Milly and the others. Instead of tents, now the fields were filled with small duplexes, new barracks, and a school. The refugee families that lived there appeared well-clothed and well-fed. Numerous children were running playfully around the grounds and mothers were casually talking to one another as they hung out their laundry.

America made her way to a large infirmary tent. Just inside the flap, she spotted a middle-aged officer sitting in a canvas chair cleaning off a surgical knife. The officer greeted her, "Hello ma'am. I'm Officer Brown. Somethin' I can help you with?"

"Yes, I'm looking for my husband," America said trying to contain her excitement.

"He's stationed here?" Officer Brown asked.

"He was. I mean, he trained here," America responded.

"Do you know what regiment he was in ma'am?"

"Hundred and fourteenth. His name is Jerry Burns."

"Oh, just a moment, ma'am," Brown said as he walked over to a ledger that was placed on a small table. He opened the ledger and scanned his finger over a list of names. He shook his head and folded his hands.

A look of concern came across his face as he braced himself to deliver bad news.

"I'm sorry ma'am. Officer Jerry Burns died about two weeks ago of consumption. He was wounded at Richmond. Made it back to camp but the illness was going around and it took him quick," Officer Brown continued.

America closed her eyes.

There was a long silence, followed by shock. America had been elated hours earlier at the news of the war's end and the hope she and Isaac would be reunited with Jerry. This terrible news struck her like a dagger. She stood there, feeling all alone in the world.

Officer Brown continued, "You should know that your husband fought honorably and faithfully, ma'am. It is men like your Jerry that changed the course of the history of our country. He did not die in vain."

"Thank you, sir," America said stoically.

Tears began to well up in America's big brown eyes. Her shoulders began to shake as she tried to compose herself and remain strong.

"Is your name America?" Brown said.

"Yes. How'd you know that was my name?" America asked through her tears.

"Jerry mentioned you. I remembered 'cause of your name—America. Jerry told his regiment he was fighting not just for the union of his country and the end of slavery but also for his own America. He wanted to make sure you got your pension. As a widow, you are entitled to an Army soldier's pension. I hope that helps you to get on from here."

America stared off into the distance. There were no words that she could say to convey her emotions.

In the tent nearby, she could hear the groan of a wounded soldier lying on a cot in pain. She looked over to observe rows and rows of young men waiting for medical care.

America composed herself before speaking again, "And his brother Charlie? Do you know what might have happened to him, Officer?"

"Charlie, you say?"

"Yes, Charles Burns."

"Can't say I know him. He was not with Jerry at the last. If he's not listed in the register as having been in need of medical care or as a fatality, he's likely with the rest of the regiment that was sent out last week to the Rio Grande, Sixty-four."

Officer Brown lifted the flap of the tent and gestured outside.

"When he returns, he will hopefully find you. Now, if you'd follow me this way, I can make sure you get your pension."

33

America - 1865 - Staying Strong

America stepped off of the stagecoach and approached the Jordan home. Outside, Lily was drawing water from a well into a wooden bucket. She looked up eagerly as America came closer. Seeing her alone, she rushed over in concern and embraced her.

America's tears began to flow again as she whispered in Lily's ear, "Jerry's gone, Lily. I'll never see him again." She wiped her eyes and pulled back from the embrace.

"I don't want him to see me cry like this, Lily," she said.

"Don't worry, he's not here right now, honey. Eli went out to the track for the day to work with the horses."

"Not Eli. Isaac," America corrected softly. "Isaac."

Lily pulled a handkerchief from her apron pocket and gently dabbed the tears from America's cheeks.

"Jerry wouldn't have wanted me to make Isaac upset or feel hopeless."

America glanced across the yard and saw her son playing, giggling, as he ran from the two Jordan girls chasing him through the clothesline.

"Isaac!" she called.

He ran to her, hiding behind her skirt.

America bent down and held him by the shoulders. He squirmed but she held fast.

"Isaac. Now you listen to me," she said seriously.

"Mommy, we was just playing!" he said, sensing the change in her voice.

"Boy, will you please listen to me?"

Lily gently gathered her daughters away to give them privacy.

"You know your Pa went to fight for our freedom and that he is a hero, don't you?"

"Yes, Mama."

"And you pray for him, don't you?"

"Yes, Mama. I always pray for Daddy."

"And every time you pray and talk to him, you need to thank him for fighting for your freedom. And you need to know that he's right there with you, walking with you, guiding you, helping you to be brave. You know that, right?"

"I know, Mama. He's always here even though he's not," Isaac said, standing tall.

Before her tears could well up again, she pulled Isaac into her and hugged him tightly. Then, she let him go.

"Go on now," she smiled and swatted him gently on the behind. He looked at her apprehensively before running back to rejoin the girls in the game again. Then she said to herself, "Go on now. Keep going."

34

America - 1869 - Solar Eclipse, August 7

Isaac and America were making it on their own now, but still living near the welcoming home of the Jordan family. The Jordans remained a source of steady moral support, especially on Sunday afternoons when America and Isaac would stop by after church services in Lexington.

America was now employed at a community laundry. Her services were in high demand, but the wages were barely enough to scrape by. Still, she worked diligently, always holding on to the hope of securing a better future for her son—one that might include a formal education.

In the warm days of August 1869, there was talk all over Lexington about an approaching total solar eclipse. America had witnessed the strange effects of lunar and solar eclipses as a child living in the slave quarters—how animals behaved oddly and the weather shifted. While some White and Black folks at the time gossiped that eclipses were signs of evil spirits or omens of the end times, America had never been particularly superstitious. She wasn't afraid to be outside during the eclipse. In fact, she wanted to embrace the experience.

She knew that her eight-year-old son, Isaac, was endlessly curious, always eager to learn. So, she decided to let him experience the eclipse in a special way. Isaac had read picture books about telescopes and science and wanted to understand more. On the morning of August 7, when the newspapers announced the eclipse's imminent arrival, crowds in Lexington began traveling to Shelbyville—a small town of 2,000 that had suddenly become a hub for astronomers.

Shelby College, a local academy chartered in 1798 for White students, owned the third-best telescope in the country. Joseph Winlock, a leading astronomer of the time and a Shelbyville native, was returning from Boston to operate the telescope. A Harvard professor who had taught at the U.S. Naval Academy and Shelby College, Winlock's homecoming made the event even more significant. Spectators flocked to the town by railcars, steamboats, carriages, and horseback to witness the spectacle. The Lexington Gazette's August 7 headline proclaimed it "The Great Astronomical Event of the Age."

America and Isaac observed the excitement in wonder. Since they had walked through the wilderness during their departure from Fort Nelson years earlier, walking a few miles to a lake near Lexington felt entirely doable.

America packed a picnic supper and a satchel of books. She placed a cap on Isaac's head and led him into nature. It was widely known that looking directly at a solar eclipse could cause eye damage, but

America had a different plan. When they reached the lake that afternoon, she instructed Isaac to look at the eclipse's reflection in the water through a piece of glass that had been smoked over a candle. She had read this was a safe method to observe it, without taking risks. The lake was crystal clear, and the vision was stunning—a shadow transforming into a crescent and then into complete darkness. The temperature dropped sharply at 4 p.m. as the sun was fully hidden, and the stars above glittered like diamonds reflected on the water's surface.

"Look, Mama!" Isaac exclaimed with awe as he viewed the eclipse through the glass piece.

"I see, son," America said, smiling. "Isn't it wonderful?"

She lit her oil lamp and pulled out the small books she had brought, wrapped in a satchel. Sitting on a blanket beside her son, she opened one to a bookmarked page and began to read aloud.

"Oh dark, dark, dark, amid the blaze of noon, irrecoverably dark, total eclipse. Without all hope of day!" she read, quoting Shakespeare. *"But fear not. It is not in the stars to hold our destiny but in ourselves."*

A silence followed as the two of them sat beneath the darkened sky. Then Isaac spoke.

"Do you think Papa sees us tonight, Mama?" he asked, his eyes searching the stars reflected in the lake.

"I believe he does see us. At least, I hope he does, Isaac."

America put her arm around her son, then reached for another small book—another by William Shakespeare.

"Romeo says in Romeo and Juliet… '*When he shall die, take him and cut him out in little stars, and he will make the face of heaven so fine that all the world will be in love with night.*'"

35

Isaac - 1884 - The First American Derby

Photo credit: Chicago Jockey Club at

Washington Park, Keystone-Mast Collection

The humid summer air was so thick it was a challenge to catch one's breath. The train pulled into Chicago and Isaac and Lucy exited the train. Isaac was heading to his mount at the first American Derby, which was to be held at Washington Park on the Windy City's South Side.

A new day was dawning in America and a new city was emerging as the hub of culture and social progress. Horse racing was the most popular sport in the country and for the first time in the county's history, a new kind of hero was emerging— a sports hero. News of these heroes traveled from person to person and through newspaper sources on the days that followed the Stakes races.

News traveled fastest to the most wealthy in society, the racing enthusiasts that ran the Jockey Clubs. They had learned that the first American Derby would be happening on June 28th in Chicago. It would be the most prestigious and highest-paying Thoroughbred race in the history of America, with a purse of $10,700.00, arranged by the newly formed Washington Park Jockey Club.

The enormous Chicago payout would be more than double what was paid for the purse that same year in the "Run for the Roses" at Churchill Downs which had been won by a twenty-three-year-old jockey named Isaac Burns Murphy on a three-year-old horse named Buchanan.

After marrying the love of his life, Lucy Carr, Isaac had gone on an unparalleled winning streak. He posted a win in the Kentucky Oaks the day before winning his first Kentucky Derby. He also won the Clark Stakes as well as his first Stakes race at Latonia. He was officially a superstar and a champion.

36

Isaac - 1884 - Racing in the Windy City

While Isaac dressed in his silks at the stables, a conversation unfolded in the Jockey Club dining room between architect Solon Spencer Beman and General Philip Sheridan.

"You've done a fine job designing the Washington Park Jockey Club," Sheridan said. "And the Roundhouse stables created by visionary architect, Daniel H. Burnham —it's unlike anything in any major city."

He continued, "When I saw your work on the Pullman neighborhood and the Studebaker building at Michigan and Van Buren, I knew we needed you. Your style has been noted by the Chicago Daily News as—Queen Anne, Romanesque Revival, Chateauesque—and it rivals the best in Europe."

Beman smiled. "That means a lot coming from you. You, Major General Sheridan, who reported directly to Ulysses S. Grant in the War. You also saved Chicago after the great fire by overseeing martial law for Mayor Roswell B. Mason. It's an honor to be in your company."

"I am glad we share the same passion for a great race," Sheridan replied. "After riding a horse in battle for so many years, I have tremendous admiration for the jockeys guiding lightning-speed

Thoroughbreds to victory. And today I am betting on the young jockey of high intelligence who appears to be on a fierce winning streak from Kentucky."

Solon nodded in agreement, "Oh yes, Isaac Burns Murphy. And he's riding a horse fit for his fine, polite manner with the press….Modesty."

"That is a grand name for a winning horse," Solon said.

Sheridan smiled. "A fine name for a fine rider."

Beman and General Sheridan bet well. Isaac rode Modesty to a stunning victory in the very first American Derby. The two distinguished gentlemen could not have been more delighted.

37

Isaac - 1884 - Lucky Makes an Entrance

Elias "Lucky" Baldwin

Photo credit: Arcadia Public Library

A flurry of horses kicked up mud as they barreled down a rural Kentucky racetrack. Isaac's head panned along with the rest of the motley crowd as the horses ran by. He was watching closely, observing their every move.

The crowd next to Isaac parted as an approaching Eli Jordan made his way through the masses.

"News of the world!" Eli exclaimed.

"What, did you buy a new cane?" Isaac laughed.

"How'd you know?" Eli said with a grin.

"Because you haven't knocked me with it yet." Isaac's eyes twinkled.

"Ah. No, Isaac. It's not about my cane. I have someone important here who'd like to meet you."

Isaac turned to see Lucky Baldwin, swaggering towards him wearing a pair of alligator skin boots and a feathered hat.

"Isaac, this is Elias Baldwin," Eli said, making a formal introduction.

Isaac turned to see a fifty-seven-year-old tall man who was "larger than life", looking down a long narrow nose at him from blue piercing eyes.

"Howdy! Call me Lucky," Lucky said as he extended a gloved hand.

The two men shook hands.

"It's a pleasure to meet you, sir," Isaac said.

Lucky spoke in a loud voice, "I've been admiring your stables from afar. I must say, I'm delighted to see you here. If I learned anything from mining it's that you find some of the most enchanting things in the most unexpected places."

As they were speaking together, a scuffle broke out in the crowd next to them.

"So what brings you here?" Isaac asked.

"I've come for my new jockey..."

Isaac looked confused as Lucky went on, "The new season is almost here and I know'd a fighter when I seen one. Ever since your suspension was over, you're back in the winner's circle. Anyone can see that," Lucky continued.

"And I'd be damned if you rode for anyone else. I didn't get my name Lucky for nothin', you know. And I had to make sure I got to you before those pigeon-livered turf-boys did," Lucky said with confidence.

"But sir, "Isaac responded, "I'm still under contract with Eli Jordan training me and deciding my mounts. It was part of the deal to bring me back to race."

They may not be Eli Jordan, Ike, but I have my own outstanding trainers in Santa Anita. Ever been?"

"No, sir," Isaac said. "Can't say I've ever been West of St. Louis."

"Well, you need to go! To a horse lover, it's paradise on earth," Lucky said as he patted Isaac on the back."The promised land, I call it. California is a bit far, sure, but I don't discriminate. I'm interested in dominating everywhere—Saratoga. Chicago, Lexington, and all over the West."

Isaac was overwhelmed.

"So, what do you say bucko? Are you ready to get Lucky with me? Cause if you keep up your winning in Chicago, I am certain you will make more money with my stables and on my mounts than you have ever seen in your life. How would you and your lovely wife like having a second home in Chicago and a third in California? I've got a three-year-old Thoroughbred named Volante that you can ride in the American Derby in 1885 that will help you earn that second house within the next few months!"

Isaac looked at Eli who smiled and nodded back reassuringly before excusing himself and making his way back through the crowd. On his way, he stopped to greet someone who appeared to be a friend. Of course, Eli had so many friends at the racetrack. He was constantly being stopped by patrons. Everyone loved Eli.

"Lookie there! Did you see that, son? Eli Jordan's given you his full approval! Scarce ever seen a man believe in someone the way that man believes in you. You must have something on him!" Lucky exclaimed.

He laughed and his eyes twinkled with excitement. But Isaac's eyes remained on Eli. He was touched by Eli's act of total selflessness. He knew that his surrogate father, "Uncle Eli" always had his best interest at heart. At one time Eli had saved not only his life, but his mother's life too.

Even if it meant losing his pride and joy, a model student and the most winning rider in his stable, Eli Jordan was encouraging Isaac to reach the highest pinnacle of excellence and expand his opportunities by moving to a place with better weather, outstanding horses, and the prospect of becoming the wealthiest and most successful athlete in America.

38

Isaac - 1885 - Second American Derby

It was 1885 and another hot day in Chicago for the second running of the American Derby. A pack of horses came flying by at lightning speed. This time, Isaac was riding a horse named Volante and wearing the racing silks of the Lucky Baldwin Stables. As he passed the post, a massive crowd of twenty thousand patrons could be seen cheering from the stands.

Isaac had become a very popular winner and fans both Black and White came from all over the country to witness him race. Lucky had struck gold once again at the racetrack with the jockey from Kentucky wearing the Baldwin white racing silks emblazoned with a black horseshoe.

Just as Lucky had predicted, Isaac would keep on winning. In 1886, he rode back into the winner's circle again with his third American Derby victory on a California horse named Silver Cloud.

It was a trifecta. Three years at the American Derby and three first-place finishes on three different three-year-old horses. Isaac Murphy was now one of the wealthiest men in America, the toast of Chicago, and an entire country of sports fans. Word of his fame was even spreading worldwide.

39

Isaac - 1886 - Isaac's Dreams for His Future

Isaac changed out of his silks in the jockey's locker room after his win on Silver Cloud and walked to the entrance of the Washington Park racetrack, joined by his best friend, Tony Hamilton. The two young men were discussing the race they had just run to a sold-out crowd of the wealthiest men and women in America.

Tony could barely contain his admiration for his closest friend, "Wow, Ike, I am proud of my second-place finish, but you—three years, three horses, three big wins. You're a legend, man. You motivate me, brother! I aim to beat your time, but you have made it nearly impossible."

"Thanks," Isaac replied. "Lucky has some great horses, and maybe he is the one bringing me the luck, or maybe it's my mom's spirit and my father's courage to put myself out there.... Whatever it is, I'm grateful."

"Can I let you in on a secret, Tony?" Isaac said with excitement. "I'm saving up to buy Lucy a beautiful home in Lexington. I want her to have the life my mother never got to have but always deserved. We want to have a fine dining room to entertain folks." Isaac's heart began racing as he spoke of his ambition, "All my life I have dreamed of having a library full of great books. I know it's a lot to ask for, but I am even dreamin' about one day owning my own mounts too."

"Your mother America is sure proud of you, Ike. I know her spirit lives in you. You are so much like her," Tony said.

"My mother was a fighter who just kept on fighting. I intend to do the same, for as long as I can. I just hope I don't get injured," Issac said.

"You and me both!" Anthony agreed.

At that moment, Lucy emerged from the grandstand at a running pace and greeted Isaac and Tony. She threw her arms around Isaac's neck and kissed him on the cheek.

"You are my hero, Isaac. I have grown to love those horses almost as much as you do. I am so hoarse from screaming for Silver Cloud that Mr. Lucky told me he was going to have to muzzle me!" She continued, "Lady—don't scream, he said, but I honestly don't care. I am so happy that you won!"

Isaac laughed. "Guess what, Luc...Lucky says we're invited to a play tonight at the Sherman Hotel. A victory party—with my friend Charles Wood's theater company entertaining us and General Sheridan in attendance! Lucky is paying for the whole shindig."

Lucy grinned. "Really? Wow, now that's the kind of luck I like!"

40

Isaac - 1886 - Charles and the Shakespeare Play

That evening, Lucy and Isaac attended a theatrical event given in Isaac's honor and a four-course dinner at the Sherman Hotel held in a fancy dining room with tablecloths, fine china and silver. It was an opulent celebration, complete with top entertainment and a mixed-race audience of Isaac Murphy fans.

Charles Winter Wood, and his acclaimed acting troupe of thespian players, composed of three beautiful and talented Black women and three handsome and talented Black men at the pinnacle of Black society in America, staged a performance that special night in the Columbia Theater.

Charles was well-known around town for his gifts as an orator and thespian. He had come to Chicago at the age of nine where he began his employment as a shoe-shine boy in Chicago's financial district. One of the prominent men Charles shined shoes for as a young man was Judge Jarvis Blume, who learned quickly that Charles had a talent for drama. Charles would recite a poem or tell a short story when requested by Judge Blume at each shoe shine.

One day Blume arrived at his shoe shine appointment and handed Charles a book of plays written by William Shakespeare. He told Charles that he would pay him a silver dollar if he could quote an entire Shakespearean soliloquy in three days when he would be back to have his shoes shined again.

Charles was up for the challenge. When Judge Blume returned, Charles gave a magnificent, fully memorized performance standing tall on the shoe shine stand, in the middle of the public financial building viewed by onlookers in awe.

Justice Blume was so impressed, that he wrote a letter to the admissions committee at Beloit College urging them to admit young Charles as an undergraduate student.

After learning his first soliloquy for the Judge, Charles became a lover of everything Shakespeare. He began reading and performing all the great Shakespearean plays and formed a theater company in Chicago.

Isaac met Charles after his second American Derby win, when the two of them, after being introduced by a friend, struck up a conversation about their mutual love of Shakespeare. It was an instant connection.

So in the summer of 1886, following Isaac's third win in the American Derby, Charles staged a performance of Richard III, with Charles playing the leading role of Richard. At the height of the play's action during the performance, Charles turned directly to Isaac and pronounced, "My horse. My kingdom for a horse," to which the entire audience erupted in thunderous applause.

Isaac had already been referred to by newsmen as "The Prince of Jockeys" for his intellect and politeness and the eloquent way he described his winning strategies in races to various members of the press.

In Chicago and throughout the country, Isaac Murphy was an example of excellence in sports and moral character. By 1886 following the American Derby, it was clear that Isaac was the undisputed "King of the Racetrack" and a star of unparalleled talent, beloved by fans of all ages and races who strived for excellence themselves. He was near the pinnacle of his racing career, and a true reflection of the hard work and values his mother America had taught him. Isaac was an inspiration to others and a hope for generations to come.

41

Isaac - 1886 - An Unexpected Encounter

After a grand night of theater and festivities in Chicago, the following evening Isaac was sitting in the back of a restaurant reading a newspaper and finishing up his meal. His traveling case was beside him. He would be heading to the station soon to meet Lucy. Lucy had gone into town earlier that day to do some shopping for their new second home in Chicago. Isaac was preparing to meet her at the platform so they could board the train out of town leaving Union Station at 7 pm sharp.

A fellow jockey passed him on the way out of the restaurant and tipped his cap to him. Isaac reacted with a smile and, "Thank you."

A few moments later, a glass of champagne was delivered by the waiter to his table, "Compliments of a Mr. King Kelly, sir," the waiter said.

Isaac looked past the waiter to the front section of the restaurant. Sitting at the bar wearing a wide-brimmed sunhat and a coat with gold buttons, King Kelly was seated. He had noticeably elevated himself to an even higher status than when Isaac last saw him.

Isaac approached King carrying his suitcase and the glass of champagne. "Much obliged to you and appreciate the compliments, sir," Isaac said to King as he walked by his table.

"Well, I expect there will be more of that to come for the 'Prince of Jockeys', my good fellow," King said as he smiled up at Isaac.

"It's nice to be back," Isaac said to King with a smile. "I must say, you appear to be doing quite well for yourself, Mr. Kelly."

"I have to look the part. I'm overseeing the financials at Sheepshead Bay these days. I fully intend to turn it into one of the finest racetracks in America, although I've got my work cut out for me after seeing this beautiful racetrack in Chicago," King said with a grin.

"Sheepshead Bay, that's a mighty investment," Isaac's eyes widened.

"Well, it takes some sticking your neck out to get anywhere. You should know something about that," King's voice got softer and he leaned closer to Isaac as though letting him in on a secret.

"I'll tell you something, Isaac. I came from nothing and no place. Didn't know my mother, and wished I never knew my father. Now I'm working for the richest men in the country. The Vanderbilts, the Belmonts, the Travers, they all turn to me for their sport. They all trust me with their fortunes. And how did I do it?"

King removed a cherry from his glass and concealed it. "They see you doing one thing with one hand, thinking they know you... while really..."

He snapped his fingers and opened his right hand, magically showing it was empty. Then he opened his left hand, revealing the cherry, "they don't."

Isaac looked puzzled, "Two cherries I take it?" he said, unsure, but venturing a guess at King's magic trick.

King smirked but did not give an answer.

"But you must ask yourself, where did he get the second one? And you, Isaac, where do you get the gumption to defy death and ride these magnificent beasts? Is it madness?"

"There's some madness, I suppose," Isaac said.

"But where does that bravery come from?" King continued as if in a trance. "See, that's the question, Isaac."

"My father was a soldier who fought for our freedom. I believe some of it comes from my father," Isaac said with pride.

King seemed a bit irritated by Isaac's answer. "My father was part of the fighting One-hundred-and-fourteenth that came out of Fort Nelson."

"So, you knew him well? This father of yours?" King asked.

"No. Wish I could have known him. He died during the war when I was very young so I don't have more than a couple of stories. My Uncle Charlie served with him and may still be alive, but we never did know what happened to him. Wish I could find my Uncle Charlie, wish I could ask him about my father. But I know that my Pa was a brave man. My earliest memory was of him lifting me up when we were living at Camp Nelson, I remember him laughing, I remember how he smelled," Isaac said, reflecting on his memory.

"And how did he smell?" King asked.

"Like pine tar and whiskey," Isaac said.

"Whiskey, huh?" King said with keen interest.

The White bartender walked over. Seeing Isaac with a champagne glass, he gave him a dirty look. King noticed this.

"Let's drink to unknown fathers," King said as he clinked his glass into Isaac's and quickly downed his entire glass.

"Enjoy the champagne. Hopefully I'll see you ride again soon enough." He stood up and patted Isaac on the arm and walked away.

"You will, sir," Isaac said as he watched him go.

42

Isaac - 1887 - Isaac's History Making Contract

Isaac was presented with a wreath of flowers and waved to an adoring crowd. At Kenner Stakes, on a different track and with a different crowd, Isaac surged to the front of a pack. Another race, another victory.

Isaac was presented with a large silver trophy. Beside him stood Lucky Baldwin with a million-dollar grin. When the race was over, Lucky put his arm around Isaac and led him into the gentleman's cigar club. After toasts with champagne flowing, the men gathered around the table with Lucky's attorney, the Honorable Fredrick Jones.

Jones placed a contract on the table and beckoned for Isaac to come over. The turfmen's faces were joyful and celebratory, many had won fortunes betting on Isaac's victories on Baldwin's mounts. Fredrick handed the document to Lucky for his signature who handed it on to Isaac along with a feather pen.

Lucky cleared his throat to make a loud announcement,

"Turfmen and horse enthusiasts of the sport, you are about to witness the signing of a jockey to my stables with the highest percentage of wins since the sport began who will now become the highest paid jockey in America!"

The crowd of men slapped each other on the back and applauded, taking in the moment being present to witness sports history.

Isaac was overcome with all the attention. He composed himself and thanked all the men present. As he exited the room, with the contract in hand, he quietly stood in the hallway to pray, "Thank you, God, and thank you, Mama and Eli, for making this possible for me." He reached in his coat pocket for the small Bible his mother had given him and ran his fingers over the binding. He recited the quote he remembered his mother teaching him, "Love does not boast or envy. It is not arrogant or rude. Love protects, hopes and perseveres. Love never ends."

Reporters and admirers flocked to Isaac as he made his way out of the cigar club towards an awaiting carriage. Reporters surrounded him with pen in hand to capture his words for the next day's newspaper. One reporter shouted out from the back of the pack, "Isaac! How does it feel to be signing the richest contract in the history of the sport? What are you going to do with all that money?"

"I still have a job to do and that's go out there and win," Isaac said. "That's what I hope to do and I'm thankful to Mr. Baldwin for giving me that chance."

Days and months passed and the victories continued. Isaac returned to Chicago and won his fourth American Derby with a silver cup riding the Emperor of Norfolk. Isaac was crowned champion for the fourth consecutive time at the Latonia Derby with a massive wreath of flowers. He plucked one off and threw it to Lucky Baldwin who stood on the rails, shouting, "Write it down, boys and girls! That's my good luck charm, Isaac Burns Murphy, the 'Prince of Jockeys'!"

Isaac - 1887 - The Superstar

Isaac entered a posh photographer's studio. "Mr. Baldwin made an appointment for me," he said to a middle-aged woman at the front desk, dressed in a white collared shirt and flowing skirt, her hair pulled high in a bun.

"Hello, Mr. Murphy. I will let Mr. Sandstrom know you are here. Can I get you a cup of coffee while you wait?"

"No thank you, ma'am."

"How about water then?"

"Yes, that would be nice. Thank you very much."

Mr. Sandstrom, a man with a cropped beard and bowler hat, emerged from another room. "Bring him water in the back room, Mrs. Drebes. Come right this way, Mr. Murphy. I am ready for you in the studio."

Isaac entered a room filled with bright lights and a single enormous camera covered by a cape.

"Please have a seat, Mr. Murphy," Sandstrom motioned. "Now just relax and pose like a U.S. President. According to the newsboys, you make more money at the track than the President himself."

He laughed at his own remark as he bent down and put his head under the cape. A loud "snap" followed.

"Well done, Mr. Murphy, well done. We'll take a couple more shots and get them over to the printing press after developing them in our dark room. Here's what your face might look like on the front of the cigarette card." He motioned to a mock-up sketch on a nearby table on a piece of cardboard. "But with the miracle of modern photography, it will be the real you and not a hand drawing."

"My mother would be happy to see this," Isaac said. "She worked as a slave for a tobacco farmer when I was a boy."

"Times certainly have changed."

"Yes, they have. Thank you kindly, sir. I hope the horse racing fans like the photo."

"You are going to be very famous indeed, Mr. Burns Murphy. Your image will be remembered throughout history."

44

Isaac - 1887 - Mansion Dreams in Lexington

Isaac and Lucy proudly looked up at their grand mansion on East Third Street in Lexington. Three movers unloaded furniture from a wagon, carrying it into the home. Two were White, one was Black.

Isaac and Lucy walked from the lawn into the house to observe the men placing their furnishings around the large front room, complete with bay windows, plush curtains and beautiful window sashes.

Lucy directed the movers as Isaac walked into the adjacent room to organize books in his new personal library. The library was massive and complete with a wooden step ladder that slid across the shelves to provide access to the full collection. Isaac opened a wooden box packed with books to place on the shelves.

As Isaac placed books on the shelves he admired each of them, especially when he came across his mother's favorites. He pondered for a few moments about all the adventures he took in his mind as a child when his mother read to him out loud and then later when he would read on his own or to her. She had taught him how to enjoy literature and value self-education through books. It dawned on him that his lifelong dream of having his own library was now a reality. And he was sharing it with Lucy. He bowed his head in gratitude and said a silent prayer.

Meanwhile, Lucy directed movers in the next room. "Thank you, gentlemen! Where are you going?"

"We finished moving in the furniture ma'am, so Mrs. Murphy, we was fixin' to head out."

"But you worked so hard for hours," Lucy said. "Come on back and stay a while with us! I baked bread this morning and was just going to put a pot of stew on the stove to eat for supper. Isaac, could you come in here and pour the men a drink? I will be back soon with food for all of us."

Hours passed as the three men conversed with the new homeowners over their dining room table, sharing stories and laughter, eating together like a family.

45

Isaac - 1889 - At the Cigar Club

Smoke hung thick in the air of a fancy private cigar club at Sheepshead Bay. King Kelly was sitting on a plush leather chair surrounded by wealthy owners, businessmen and politicians. Among them were Thomas Blackburn, William R. Travers, Pierre Lorillard IV and Leonard Jerome.

Jerome spoke first, "It would seem as though there's a new breed of person these days; celebrity."

"Indeed," Lorillard responded. "The biggest among them is in this very sport. You are no doubt referring to the Kentucky boy with the Irish last name. Well, he may be talented, or whatever you want to call it, but it's the horse's doing. He's been lucky. I dare say, the horses he rides were mostly bred by the stable that raised them in California."

Travers jumped in the conversation, "Interesting choice of words there, Lorillard. Are you ready to admit that the cowboy, Lucky Baldwin, is formidable?"

King stood up and paced before them.

"Gentlemen, it's not just riding with Lucky Baldwin. Whether it's Williams or Hunt-Reynolds or Corrigan, the name atop the horse stays the same. It's impossible to deny that Isaac Burns Murphy is the greatest aboard we've ever seen," King said, stating a fact.

"Better than old Abe?" Belmont chimed in.

"There's no doubt. The competition is much fiercer these days," King said as he inserted the cigar back in his mouth.

"He's no better than Fred Archer. He's the 'Colored Archer' maybe," Belmont countered.

King's response was swift: "I say he's much better than Archer."

"I have it. Snapper Garrison," Lorillard spoke out as he snapped his fingers. "Besides the fluke at Monmouth seasons ago, Snapper's won far more important races than Murphy."

"Snapper is better," Blackburn agreed.

"Still…," Travers joined the others, "Murphy's one of the most famous men in America. An athlete and a colored man!"

"Let them have their athletics," Blackburn smirked. "Their kind is closer to the animal anyway."

"Murphy's a fine man," Belmont remarked. "I've spent time with him. Very courteous. He's not like the rest of the riff-raff he comes from."

"Hmm. An exception to the rule no doubt," Blackburn replied as he puffed out his chest and adjusted his seat.

King took a long drag off of a cigar, not bothering to defend.

Lorillard leaned forward, "Anyway, it will all soon be settled. Pulsifier has asked for a match race."

All the men perked up with keen interest.

"What!?" Belmont asked.

"Salvator versus Tenny, " Lorillard continued. "The two greatest horses of our time, head-to-head."

"And the jockeys?" Blackburn inquired.

All of the men leaned further forward.

"Who else?" Lorillard said. "The best White jockey matched against the best colored jockey. No doubt, the race of the century."

46

Isaac - 1889 - At the Haggin Mansion

Isaac stepped down from a carriage and approached the Ben Ali Haggin Estate, a towering Second Empire mansion. A Black maid answered the door, overcome with excitement to be the one inviting Isaac Murphy into the home. She took his coat and directed him into a large drawing room.

Isaac entered and looked towards the lofted ceiling and then down the wide hall. At the other end, Lucky sat in a chair next to a short and portly man in a velvet three-piece suit, Ben Ali Haggin. Haggin was a man in his fifties, another mining tycoon, and one of the wealthiest men in the United States. As soon as they saw Isaac, both men stood up.

"There's the man," Lucky said, announcing Isaac's entrance.

The corpulent man shook Isaac's hand. "Isaac Burns Murphy. The most famous sportsman in America. My name is Ben Ali Haggin."

"Mr. Haggin, I am pleased to meet you," Isaac said, extending a firm handshake.

"Ben's an old friend of mine, and an old enemy, but mostly a friend," Lucky said with a wink.

Haggin' spoke rapidly, "I've never seen Lucky so plumb mad to lose something, let alone a jockey. But he came my way once he saw what you're about to see. JT Pulsifier believes he has a horse that can beat my Salvator. He's wagering a hundred thousand dollars on it. Twenty thousand is the prize."

Isaac looks stunned. "That's got to be…"

Lucky interrupted him mid-sentence, "The richest match race of all time, yes."

"That's remarkable. Have they picked a track?" Isaac asked.

"There's a bidding war going on as we speak," Haggin continued, "but we're leaning towards Sheepshead."

Isaac didn't know what to say.

Lucky smiled broadly "This is it, Isaac. This is the big one. It's Snapper. Pulsifier's chosen Snapper Garrison to be his jockey on Tenny. And we want you to mount Salvator."

47

Isaac - 1889 - One Star Meets Another

Isaac, Lucky, and Haggin walked through the gardens to a private stable. As they neared the entry doors, they were met by a lanky Irish horse trainer, Matt Byrnes, a man in his forties, filled with eccentric energy.

All four of the men observed a young White stable boy with fiery red hair leading a horse out from one of the stalls. Into the light stepped a dark, ferocious-looking stallion with the composure and might of a mythical beast.

Byrnes introduced the horse to the men as though he were addressing a King.

"This is the great Salvator."

Isaac gazed at the Thoroughbred with stunned admiration.

"If he isn't magnificent, I don't know what is," Byrnes said.

Haggin turned to Isaac, "Sired by Prince Charlie. He's got the blood of Lexington in him. On his dam's side, the line stretches back to Diomed. This horse is bred for nothing but speed."

Isaac ran his hands along the body of the horse, making his way towards the muzzle. He took a moment to look deep into Salvator's eyes. Then, as if asking the horse...

"May I?" Isaac inquired. "By all means," Haggin answered.

Byrnes led the horse further out into the sunshine adjacent to the training track. Isaac nimbly swung himself into the saddle. Even though he was dressed in a business suit, the horse sensed Isaac's skill and desire. With a soft nudge from Isaac's boot, the horse and rider took off in a dash across the track out of the rails and into the larger estate, winding their way along the sweeping grounds as if they were floating on air. The three men on the ground observed in awe. Isaac's command of Salvator was immediate.

Isaac and Salvator flew across Haggin's property, turning through a canopy of trees, past fountains and gardens. Isaac took the horse further across the fields until coasting to a stop to admire the distant roll of Arcus clouds far off on the horizon. He tapped his pocket to feel for his mother's small Bible to make sure it was riding along with him. Horse and rider looked out as though gazing into the future.

"We're going to ride for America, Salvator," Issac said to the stallion. "She's going along with us and I believe we can win."

48

America - 1870 - Inspiration from Literature

America slid a wet cloth across a dirty window in the Paxton estate, one of three homes she currently cleaned. She bent over a dusty floor in the back entranceway to the maid's quarters, scrubbing a patch of dried mud with a brittle brush. She completed her daily duties and went to a burly White man with a scruffy beard handing out the wages for house workers. He wiped his brow and nose and reached into a register to retrieve a few coins. He placed them in America's worn, brown hand.

She accepted the coins gratefully, curtsied, removed her apron, and departed. When she arrived home, she took off her modest coat, bent down, and lifted a floorboard in the corner of her small one-room house. Underneath the board, she removed a soup can, opened the lid, and stashed the coins.

Years passed and America kept working and saving, a few coin wages at a time. She cooked and cleaned for three affluent families, the Paxtons, Pruitts and Johnsons. After work in their mansions, she came home and cooked and cleaned her own small home. Every night she returned from work, she repeated the vigil, placing as many pennies in the floorboard can as possible. Her savings were growing.

A young neighbor girl named Pamela who America had taught reading and writing lessons on Saturdays walked across the street from her own small one-room house and kept watch over Isaac during most of America's working hours. Isaac played with the neighborhood children and helped stock shelves of canned goods and boxes for the Black grocer up the street. He made a tiny amount of money for his effort and was allowed to use it as his allowance. Whenever he wasn't working, he spent quiet hours reading.

At night when America put Isaac to bed, she would read aloud to him by the oil lamp. She brought books home from the Lexington Community Library and left them by his small bed; picture books, adventure books, stories of treasure, and books written by famous authors. And each night she would read Isaac passages from her tiny Bible, the one she kept in her bag the night Eli had rescued them from the boarding house.

Isaac particularly loved the Psalms, the stories in the Bible he learned first at Camp Nelson about Jonah and the whale, Noah, and the Ark, The Prodigal's Son, and Joseph's coat of many colors. America kept him healthy and encouraged him to play hopscotch and jacks and games outdoors with other boys that lived nearby, staying in close range of Pamela in the safety of their Black neighborhood, the tenement row houses in Lexington.

One night she came home from work and found Isaac reciting Shakespeare out loud, *"To be or not to be,"* he said as he stood proudly on his bed. *"That is the question."* After making this statement, he jumped down off his perch before approaching his mother at the coat rack, "I've decided I am going to be like Hamlet, Mama. Or maybe I will be a Musketeer!" He pretended to sword fight, with an imaginary weapon.

America smiled, "You are funny, just like your daddy was, and I know you have big dreams." Her tone changed as she looked deep into Isaac's eyes. "But always remember what the Bible says in Proverbs 16: 18-19, *Pride goeth before a fall.* So son, keep a careful watch out not to be too proud. Instead, listen, work hard, and always do your best. Never lie, cheat, steal or wish bad luck on anybody out of jealousy or greed. And you will bring Glory to God. That is the goal you should strive for. Now wash up and get ready for supper."

49

America - 1872 - Freedman's Bank Deposit

America and Isaac washed and dressed in their finest clothes, and stood together at the Freedman's bank desk as America emptied the savings from her soup can. A Black teller wearing a professional dark suit asked America to fill out paperwork. Isaac observed the transaction and conversation between America and the clerk, staring up at them in wonder.

"And here, for remarks, am I required to put down anything?" America asked.

"You can indicate those other persons using the account," the lady replied.

"No one to draw but myself and when he is grown, my son, Isaac Murphy Burns," America said as she gestured to Isaac beside her.

"Good. Well Missus Murphy Burns, thank you for opening an account at the Freedman's Savings and Trust Company."

When the paperwork was complete, America left the bank feeling quite content that Jerry's pension and her hard-earned savings, penny by penny, now lay the foundation for a brighter future for mother and son.

50

America - 1872 - A New Job Offer

Outside America's home, she heard the sound of hoofbeats. America went to the window and looked outside to see an approaching Eli Jordan on horseback. He tied up his horse and knocked on the door.

"Well if it isn't Mr. Jordan!" said America in a cheerful voice. "Making quite an entrance you are, riding up on another beautiful horse. How are you? Isaac, come over and give your Uncle Eli a big hug. Can I get you something to eat? How are Lily and the girls?"

"We're all right, Meccie, but we miss you and the boy," Eli said with kind eyes. "My work keeps me busy you know and I actually really enjoy it, 'specially the training of my stable boys."

Without a word, America offered Eli hot coffee and a biscuit. He removed his hat and set his cane down by the coatrack and sat at the table.

"Thank you most kindly, America," Eli said as he accepted her offerings.

America sat beside him after pulling up another chair for Isaac and bringing over cups and a coffee pot from the stove. Isaac came over, hugged Eli and politely took a seat next to him.

Eli leaned forward, "I came to visit you today, because I may have a job for you that's a good one."

America grinned and looked at Isaac, "That so? Well, I've got three jobs right now."

"I know how hard you work but this job I have in mind for will pay you more. It's the same work but much less hopping around," Eli said as he took a sip of the hot coffee.

"I'm getting along fine, Eli. I've been workin' for three different White families on the East side and with the money I've earned, and Jerry's pension, I just opened an account at the Freedman's," America said with a confident grin.

"Ah, so all's well and good. Sounds like you don't need to know then."

Eli stood up and put on his hat as if signaling to leave.

"Goodbye! And have a great night."

America stopped him, "Alright, Eli, spill it."

Eli turned to America, looking directly in her eyes. "My employer, Mr. Williams of Williams and Owings Stables is in need of a new full-time housemaid. They entertain quite a bit and the house is nice with plenty of rooms. Williams can be a bit hard-nosed but he respects good work and he's decent and his wife is kind. I told him about you and rode straight away to see if you were up for it."

America smiled broadly, excitement twinkling in her eyes. "Did My Pa save your life or something?"

The sarcasm continued as Isaac's eyes darted back and forth watching his mother and Eli kid each other.

"Green Murphy? Save my life?" Eli said, raising his eyebrows.

Eli laughed.

"In a manner of speaking, I suppose Green Murphy did save my life."

"Once again, Eli, you are too kind to me." America said blushing.

Eli looked over at Isaac. "It's the boy I'm after. I've had my eye on him since the first time I saw him. Johnny at the market tells me he's smart and strong for his small size, has a bright disposition and works very hard. He's going to be a great jockey someday."

Isaac beamed with pride sitting up straight in his small chair.

America responded quickly and affectionately. "Now, Eli, don't put any ideas in his head. I want him focused on reading and learning so he can someday go to a proper school."

"Alright, alright. Tomorrow morning I will send a cart and horse to take you to tell the other families you are no longer working for them and get you over to Williams' home before sundown," said Eli. "You'll be ready at 6 am? "

America smiled, "Yes, Eli, I'll be ready."

51

America - 1872 - Williams Manor and Stables

America entered the regal home of James Williams adorned with oak paneled walls, crystal chandeliers, and large portraits of horses. America circulated the rooms, admiring the decor. She stopped in front of one large painting that caught her eye. It was an oil painting of a reddish horse tended to by a Black trainer and Black stable hand.

America scrutinized the regal horse and the faces in the painting; subservient and void of emotion. She pondered its meaning and remembered her own father, Green Murphy, a bell ringer and a horse auction crier who she would sometimes accompany from the stable to the auction. Her father had a strong voice and a kind heart. She admired and adored him. She smiled as she entertained her childhood memories and then moved on. But looking back at the painting, she caught the sight of her own reflection in a nearby mirror. She continued working through her duties.

52

Isaac - 1890 - Weighing In, Curbing Hunger

Photo credit: Salvator, Keeneland Library

Hemment Collection

A scale stood in a prone position when suddenly the arm shot up indicating that a weight had been applied over one hundred and fifteen pounds. A hand slid the scale around, adjusting the measurement until it balanced on a readout correctly, to calculate the weight of the person being measured as one hundred and twenty-one.

Isaac stood there, looking at his readout, disappointed and concerned. The year was 1890 and Isaac had just won his second Kentucky Derby. Edward West, the young stable boy who was tending to a horse in a nearby stall, heard the sound of a rider throwing up.

He leaned out of the stall to see Isaac walking down the row wiping his mouth with the back of one hand while a bottle of champagne was swinging in the other.

Edward admired Isaac and wanted to protect him. He had heard rumblings as the horses were being led out to and from races by angry White jockeys cursing about Isaac's success, vowing to bring him down and beat him at the racetrack.

"Are you sick, Ike?" Edward inquired. "If you are, should you be drinkin' before the race?"

Isaac laughed and uncorked the champagne, a little weary but clearly not drunk or even tipsy.

"I learned this from Oliver Lewis, Ed. He told me that a little splash of champagne helps." He took a modest sip from the bottle. "It helps with the hunger."

Isaac passed Edward the bottle before continuing, "Ginger ale also does the trick. So I prefer that but I've got to be under one fifteen to mount Salvator. This stallion—he's unlike anything I've ever seen. I've got to ride that horse. I feel like we were meant for each other."

"He's meaner than you," Edward said.

Isaac smiled, "I can be mean."

Edward shook his head, "Out there maybe. But Ike, the bigger and more famous you get, the more they want to hurt you."

53

Isaac - 1890 - A Photographic Marvel

Inside one of the grandest racetracks in the Northeast, a group of the wealthiest men in America gathered underneath a banner that read: SALVATOR V. TENNY.

Before the crowd, standing on a small platform, was King Kelly. Isaac stood on the periphery, watching the affair.

"Gentlemen! Welcome!" Kelly barked to the crowd like a politician making a famous speech. "I couldn't be prouder that you've chosen Sheepshead Bay for this monumental race. Now if you'll oblige me, I'd like to show you a new feature of our Circus Maximus."

King pointed up to a strange photographic contraption being assembled at the top of the grandstands by John C. Hemment.

"That camera mounted at the top of the stands," King continued, "is outfitted with a dark room for quick developing. An image can be processed there in under forty-five seconds. It's a new technology never used before that we are introducing for the first time. A 'photo finish' as it were."

The men all murmured to one another in admiration. As the crowd of men gathered in the catered owner's section, King Kelly made his way over to Isaac who he saw standing at a distance.

"Ike! Might I see you for a moment? I'd like to show you something," King said as he led Isaac into the Chairman's Office. It was a grand room with large curtained windows that looked out onto the owner's section. "Can I offer you a drink?"

Isaac's answer was quick, "No, thank you."

"Aw, come now. Have a whiskey," King urged.

King opened up a liquor cabinet and poured a whiskey.

"You're a great champion, Isaac. A true winner through and through. You're much of the reason why all this is happening."

King handed Isaac the whiskey drink he had just poured.

"I'm sure at this point you're used to being the favorite."

"I don't really see it that way, Mr. Kelly," Isaac humbly replied. "Every race is a new race. I have to trust the horse and the horse has to trust me. And I have to know the other horses and riders to guide my horse the right way to the finish."

"You're too polite," King gushed and continued, "All are anticipating a close contest but most are pinning their bets on the boy from Kentucky. These men..."

King rolled a golden paperweight over his desk.

"Wealth beyond wealth. Power beyond power. All believing that they stand alone. Many former Confederates, men who fought against your father, they profit off of you, plunder your wins. And they pay you, but not nearly what you're worth. It's time they were shown who holds the reins."

"Salvator has what it takes, of that I'm certain, sir," Isaac said with confidence.

"Enough with the modesty. I'm not talking about the damn horse!" King said, frustrated that Isaac was not responding to his compliments.

"Then, what are you talking about?" Isaac inquired.

"I want to do something for you, Isaac but I'd need to know if you would go for it," said King as he once again began to roll the gold paperweight on the desk. "I have a particular connection that means to wager almost a half million on this race."

"A half a million?" Isaac nearly dropped the glass he was holding of which he had not taken a sip.

"That's right. And I could secure a good share of that for you. But they want to run the bet counter to Salvator, Isaac..."

King leaned in and spoke softly, "Ease back tomorrow and you'd ring up the lot of them. Ease back tomorrow and you'd show them what you're really worth."

"You want me to throw the race?" Isaac said, his ears getting hot and his temper rising.

"I know who you are Isaac. You're honorable, decent, you never step out of line. The world's their stage and you've played your part for them. Be modest, hold your tongue, don't fight back. Real honor, you already have that. You've already won. Salvator is already the greatest horse that ever lived and you are already the greatest jockey there ever was. It's not about winning out there. It's about winning in here."

He motioned to the next room, "Money. The real game." King's hand returned to the gold paperweight. "The real race. Amounts of money which would be enough to buy your own horses. Not the left-over nags, but champions that can sire more champions. Run your own stables, run under your own colors. Think of it..."

King put his arm around Isaac and pointed down to the track.

"You, an owner, seeing your own horses dominate the turf. A man like you, finally in control. A colored man like no other."

Isaac looked up, as if searching for guidance above him. After a moment, he reclaimed a still command...

"I've played my part as all men do. But I know who I am."

"Not the way I see it, Isaac," King said.

"Well then, you don't know me, Mr. Kelly," Isaac replied with closure.

King was not ready to give in, "I don't have to. All I have to know is what you're up against. Why do you ride Isaac? I'll tell you why. It's the only way they'll look at you."

"Play their game and you'll never be enough. Never any more than a jockey," King went over to the window and pointed at the crowd of turfmen. "Never any more than a colored man. Never any more than a slave. You know this..."

Isaac looked at the crowd.

"Look at them, Isaac. This is your chance, your chance to show them, to take what's really yours," King coaxed, almost in a dream state.

Isaac took a long hard look at the crowd of pompous, White men in their finery, talking over property and power.

"Think about it," King said.

Isaac started to leave the office, but as soon as he set down the whiskey glass, he stopped. He felt for the small Bible in his pocket before responding.

"I never intend to lose, Mr. Kelly, and I won't," Isaac stated as he exited the door, stunned and still processing the conversation that had just taken place in the Chairman's office. As he walked out, he took one more look across the balustrade to the owners' section and the wealthy, White men talking about their possessions and victories and shook his head.

"Mama, I will honor you all the days of my life," he said under his breath.

54

Isaac - 1890 - A Newsman for the Ages

Onto a steam-filled platform at the Boston Railway Station stepped the spectacled T. Thomas Fortune, a prominent Black activist and newspaperman who was the founder of the newspaper, *The New York Age.* He took off his glasses and rubbed free the mist before putting them back on to read a sign for: Sheepshead Bay.

Thomas was born into slavery himself, in Marianna, Jackson County, Florida. He started learning at the very first school established by African Americans after the Civil War. He worked for various papers as a young boy and became interested in journalism and law and was passionate about government and justice.

Thomas started his first newspaper job in New York City but left to attend Howard University in Washington D.C. He wanted to make a difference in the fight for African American Civil Rights and took on leadership roles in various organizations, working eventually with Booker T. Washington and Ida B. Wells. At the time of the "Great Race" between Isaac Murphy and Snapper Garrison, Thomas was running his own newspaper and had a keen interest in the advancement of colored people.

Fortune looked up at the monumental entrance to the Sheepshead Bay racetrack that day and the thousands of people flocking towards it. He turned to his good friend, Frank, a handsome Black man in his thirties, standing beside him.

"To think that all these people are coming to see someone who looks like us," Thomas remarked in delight.

"Not your cynical self today, Tom?" Frank replied with a grin.

"*The New York Age* isn't all desolation, Frank," Thomas remarked. "But it's a shame that we find ourselves at the racetrack and not also in the halls of government."

"That's the spirit," Frank's grin got even bigger.

Fortune looked up at the racetrack sign again, "Progress requires truth my friend, and the truth hurts."

"Well the truth is these tickets were very hard to get, so you're required to enjoy yourself," said Frank, with a chuckle.

"I plan to do exactly that!" Thomas replied. "And if my name carries any weight, maybe I will get to interview him."

"Knowing your drive, I have no doubt you will make it happen," Frank remarked with assurance.

Thomas and Frank entered the racetrack grounds and took their seats in packed grandstands that were buzzing with anticipation. Fortune looked out at the crowd, the electric environment stripping away his usual stoicism.

The excitement reached a fever pitch as Isaac, riding Salvator, and Snapper riding Tenny, made their way out onto the track and toward the starting line.

Fortune inched forward in his seat. "This is going to be a great day. I can feel it," he said with confidence.

As the jockeys came close to one another, Isaac looked over at Snapper and nodded his head as a kind gesture. Snapper looked back expressionless. Although they had met at the racetrack before, this time Snapper glared down at his competition, his eyes fierce, filled with the desire to win at all costs.

It was clear this was going to be a fight to the finish. Isaac tapped his pocket to make sure his mother's Bible was secure for the race. He said a silent prayer as he entered the gate, then leaned into Salvator's ear and whispered, "Remember, Salvator, we are riding for America."

The starter raised his gun...

BANG!

Both horses jumped from the post in synchronization.

In a near instant, they reached the first furlough where Isaac was guiding Salvator's tremendous strides into an early lead.

The horses ran the quarter mile in twenty-five seconds. Then Isaac pushed Salvator, increasing the pace.

At the half, Isaac glanced back to see Tenny and Snapper slipping nearly two lengths behind. He took Salvator and cut to the rail, looking like an easy winner if he could just hold on.

But around the far turn, with an eighth of a mile to go, Snapper began whipping his whip on Tenny's withers in an absolute fury. Tenny responded, charging bravely.

Gaining... Gaining...

Isaac looked back over his shoulder to the outside. Garrison and Tenny rushed with near impossible speed. The challenger seemed to have a burst of energy that Salvator lacked.

Isaac leaned into his horse, but Tenny and Snapper were too much. Soon enough they were...

Racing, absolutely neck-and-neck. The two horses were riding along together, pushing each other. Both jockeys were straining in their saddles, watching as the finish line drew closer.

Tenny seemed to take the edge, then Salvator... And then...

They crossed.

55

Isaac - 1890 - The Match Race of the Century

The patrons in the grandstands at Sheepshead Bay gasped and looked at each other with a mixture of confusion, shock and surprise.

Fortune stood on top of his seat. Even those seated close to the finish line had no idea who won the race or if it was a dead tie.

Snapper Garrison and Isaac Murphy looked at one another as they slowed their pace past the finish line.

"I beat you!" Snapper yelled at Isaac. Isaac remained silent and stoic.

Two different owner's boxes, both Haggin's and Pulsifier's, seemed convinced of their victories. They were both claiming the win and talking in loud voices amongst themselves.

King Kelly looked at the track in consternation, wanting to believe that Isaac had purposely pulled back at the last few seconds, but he couldn't be sure. King turned to the top of the grandstands where...

John C. Hemment emerged from the makeshift darkroom next to the elaborate camera set-up. He lifted the first-ever sports photo finish high into the air and announced:

"I declare the winner in this historical photograph. Salvator by a nose!"

The stands of patrons and racing enthusiasts erupted in applause. People clamored to get a look at the photograph which clearly showed Isaac and Salvator just ahead of Snapper and Tenny as they came across the finish line.

Fortune, Frank and large portions of the grandstands jumped up and down and cheered in a state of euphoria.

Reporters and fans pushed through the gates in a frenzy and onto the track. They began shouting questions toward Isaac as he dismounted.

"Come on," Frank said to Fortune, "Let's go!"

A reporter from a top New York paper shouted through the crowd, "Isaac, how does it feel to have run and won the greatest race of all time?"

Another reporter chimed in, "Isaac! Did you know Salvator was going to win? Did you plan that finish?"A third reporter pushed into Isaac's earshot, "Isaac, how does it feel to make history today?"

Fortune squeezed his way through the throngs, the only Black newsman present. Isaac saw him and nodded in his direction.

"Mr. Murphy! T. Thomas Fortune of the *New York Age!*" Fortune exclaimed.

Isaac smiled from ear to ear. Recognition and pride washed over him, seeing the nation's most prominent Black newsman.

"Mr. Fortune! Good to see you, sir. I admire your editorials!"

"You've made quite an example out there, Ike," Fortune responded.

"Thank you, Thomas. It was fast and that's how Salvator likes it."

"You favor close races it seems," Fortune observed.

"Close or not, there's only one thing that matters in racing—Winning"

As Isaac was swept away by the crowd, Fortune called after him.

"Mr. Murphy! One more question!"

Isaac looked back at Fortune. The two men locked eyes.

"Why do you ride?"

"I ride to win," Isaac said matter-of-factly. "And I ride for my mother, America."

With that, Isaac was quickly whisked away by admirers. Fortune took a moment and allowed Isaac's words to sink in. He would write Isaac's famous quote in his next editorial.

There was no way to describe the joy that day for the Isaac Burns Murphy fans far and wide. And when the newspapers announced the winner of the "Match Race of the Century" the following day on every printing press coast to coast and around the world, the joy spread far and wide. Hemment's photograph would become the first official "photo finish" in American sports history.

56

Isaac - 1890 - Haggin Mansion Celebration

Champagne bottles exploded. A massive crowd of the richest of the rich was gathered inside the gaudy Kentucky mansion belonging to James Ben Ali Haggin. They were attending an extravagant celebration. Haggin stood at the helm of the crowd.

He raised a glass and addressed those gathered about him,

"To Isaac Murphy, the greatest jockey this side of the Atlantic, we have a very special trophy."

A gloved butler named Randal handed Haggin a silver-mounted whip.

Haggin continued his announcement, "A silver whip! It reads: 'Salvator verses Tenny, Champion Jockey Isaac Burns Murphy.'"

A cheer rang through the hall as Isaac stepped forward to accept his prize.

"Now gentlemen, let's celebrate!" Haggin pointed to Issac, "I don't want to see that man with an empty glass tonight!"

The party rolled on. Isaac seemed to be genuinely enjoying himself, constantly being talked to by the White wealthy men, acting polite. Every time his glass was below full, it was filled to the brim by the roaming wait staff serving champagne and whisky from silver trays. Haggin tapped a few VIPs on the shoulder. He beckoned them to follow him, "Come right this way, Gents. I want to give you a tour of my residence."

Haggin led Isaac and the select group on a private tour of his mansion. After walking through the upstairs wing and main floor, they stepped down into a large wine cellar where hundreds of bottles lined a maze of shelves.

Haggin pointed to the bottles, "Name a country and it has a vintage here." As he spoke, King Kelly glanced down the stairs and observed that Isaac was part of the tour in the wine cellar. He descended the stairs to get closer to him.

Haggin noticed King coming down to join the larger group. "Kelly, you devil!", he called out to him. "Truly I couldn't think of a better arena than Sheepshead. Well done."

"Thank you, Ali," King responded as he altered his position to get right beside Isaac. "Oh— Isaac!" King said as he handed Isaac a full wine glass, "You'll have to try this. Haggin tells me it's the vintage of kings, so I assume it'd be fit for a prince."

"Yes," Haggin agreed, "one of the finest in our cellar. Give it a go, Ike."

The butler opened the bottle and poured Isaac another very full glass. Isaac's head was beginning to spin, but he kept his composure. Haggin became distracted by another party guest and began leading the others in another direction. Isaac prepared to leave when he was stopped by King. "Isaac, I would like to speak to you privately," King said.

Isaac turned away, wary. He remembered their last encounter at Sheepshead all too well. He had won the tight match, which was not the outcome King urged him to accept the afternoon before the race when the two men spoke in the Chairman's office.

"That race was one hell of a show," King remarked.

"I did what I had to do, Mr. Kelly," Isaac said as he looked King directly in the eyes. "I hope you understand that."

"I'm quick to learn," King countered.

"Good evening, sir," Isaac toasted him before setting the full wine glass down on a nearby table and then, moving to depart King's company.

"Before you go, Ike, as a gesture of good feeling between us, there's someone I'd like you to meet. Don't ask me how I was able to track him down but I knew, more than anything, you'd like to speak to him. You said your father was in the One-hundred-and-fourteenth Regiment of the United States Colored Infantry?"

Kelly whistled and snapped at the butler, Randal, cleaning up glasses left in the wine cellar. "Fetch him," he ordered Randal.

King turned to face Isaac, "It took some doing...but...."

Randal returned with a diminutive Black man in his fifties, who was dressed in a suit that didn't quite fit him. He looked nervously at King.

"Yess'm," the man spoke, as if answering a command. "Yes?"

"Isaac, this is your Uncle Charlie," King said.

A rush of complete surprise came over Isaac. He had consumed sips of several alcoholic drinks at the party and was totally unprepared to receive this news.

Isaac searched the man's face, stunned, trying to place the recognition of his Uncle Charlie from over two decades before. "Uncle Charlie?" said Isaac in disbelief.

"That's me. It's your Uncle," Charlie said.

Isaac didn't know what to say. Charlie extended his arms out, waiting for Isaac to embrace him. After a moment, Isaac did so emphatically and exclaimed.

"My God! I thought I'd never see you again! Praise the Lord! My mother America hoped you would come back someday!"

King seemed very pleased, winked at Charlie and backed away, "I'll leave you two be." He began walking up the steps from the cellar to the main house, leaving the two men alone at the bottom of the stairs. There was a long silence before Charlie spoke again.

"You look just as I remember," he said.

"And you… well the last time I saw you was one of my earliest memories, that time when you and Pa marched out of Camp Nelson."

"Sure, sure," Charlie nodded his head in response.

"Uncle Charlie, where have you been all this time? Mama said you went to Texas but she thought you must have died out there?"

"Ah, it's been a long road. I… I traveled 'round the West a bit. But I got word you become a great rider and I come to see you," Charlie said as he wiped his nose with the back of his hand.

Isaac spoke again almost out of breath, "All this time I was hoping and praying to find the one person who could tell me about my Pa. I always heard he was full of humor and was a very brave soldier."

There was a pause and Charlie made a peculiar facial expression, wrinkling his brow and distorting his face before speaking again.

"Your Pa was a very funny man. Very funny. Always laughing, always joking. But brave?….na…..". A chuckle escaped his lips.

He hesitated, before saying more,

"If you want to know the truth, he wasn't brave none. Could scarce go into battle without a stiff drink. Had to drink himself into a daze to muster the courage. Always drinkin' and even then, he didn't want to fight. No."

Charlie took a long drink himself and once again rubbed his runny nose with the back of his hand.

"Runs in the family, I guess. World's cruel and ain't nothin' we can do about it except try to forget it from time to time," he said as he hung his head.

Charlie laughed a sickly laugh. Isaac stared off into the distance, clearly rattled.

"So tell me about ridin'. I hear them Jockey Clubs can get pretty wild, huh? How about the ladies? I bet you have a few of them after you all the time and you'd be gettin' lucky…." A sinister smile left his lips as he took another long drink.

Isaac remained quiet, saddened by the news about his father and not sure what to say to his father's brother, the only living connection he had to his own paternal roots and past. After composing himself, Isaac spoke again.

"Where do you live now, Charlie? Are you in Lexington? I want to give you a lift home and arrange a time soon when you can meet my wife, Lucy, and join us for dinner. Come with me upstairs so I can get my coat and say good night to the others."

"Oh, no," Charlie said, dropping his head and looking away. He hung back as Isaac began to go up the stairs. "I'd better go out the back way. Don't think I belong up there."

Isaac returned his gaze with kind eyes, "Whatever you prefer. I will get my coat and we can both go out the back way. Please excuse me for just a moment while I thank the host."

Isaac nodded and continued up the stairs. After expressing his gratitude to Haggin for the gift and festivities, he returned to the basement wine cellar to find it empty. Uncle Charlie had vanished into the night, leaving the back door to the cellar ajar.

Isaac opened the door and called out into the darkness, "Uncle Charlie? Uncle Charlie?" The night was silent and there was no response. Isaac shook his head and climbed the stairs again. It was almost as though he had imagined the whole encounter with his Uncle Charlie, but at the same time, it was chillingly real.

Isaac emerged from the cellar once again. But something was now haunting him. In the midst of the continuing party, for some reason, he sensed extreme danger.

As he wound his way through the party heading toward the front door, he entered the drawing room where a rapt audience was now listening to the gregarious vaudeville actor, DeWolf Hopper, performing a tipsy poem.

"'Fraud!' cried the maddened thousands, and the echo answered, 'Fraud!' But one scornful look from Casey and the audience was awed."

Isaac watched as DeWolf stood up dramatically on a chair.

"Somewhere in this favored land the sun is shining bright, the band is playing somewhere, and somewhere hearts are light, and somewhere men are laughing, and somewhere children shout, but there is no joy in Mudville... mighty Casey has struck out!" DeWolf shouted as the entire rapt audience burst into laughter and applause.

Isaac moved to the door and climbed into a carriage out front. He instructed the man behind the reins to go to the cellar door entrance around back to have one more look for another passenger before taking him home. Finding no one there, he asked the driver to continue on. The carriage wound its way through the streets as Isaac stared off into the distance. Once back at his residence, he tipped the driver, thanked him, and walked up the front steps.

Isaac entered his home in a bit of a stupor, closing the door behind him loudly. He hung his coat on the rack and placed his new silver whip in the umbrella stand beside it. He sat down on the foyer sofa, and concern and worry lined his face. After breathing deeply, he lifted his hands to cover his face in despair.

Lucy appeared at the top of the staircase, dressed in a nightgown.

"Isaac? You alright?" Lucy said with concern.

Not hearing an answer, she headed down the stairs.

"I told you there's no need to stay at these things. They wear you out," Lucy observed Isaac hanging his head.

His voice was soft-spoken. "Something bad is going on Luc," he said.

"With what? What's the matter?" Lucy replied, comforting her husband. "You just won the 'Match Race of the Century', Isaac."

"Something is off, Lucy, I can feel it," he continued.

Lucy sat beside him and hugged him on the sofa.

"Isaac, you need to get some rest. Come on upstairs."

Isaac's voice was filled with worry, "There's only one more race this season. One more ride on Salvator. I can't let anything happen to him, Lucy. I must protect him."

Salvator verses Tenny, "Match Race of the Century"

Photo credit: Keeneland Library Hemment Collection

57

Isaac - 1890 - Stables by Night

Carrying a lantern, Isaac walked through the dark stables and entered Salvator's stall. Before Isaac stood the majestic horse, seemingly untouched. Isaac brushed his hide, breathing a sigh of relief.

"I'm going to look after you, Salvator," he said softly in the stallion's ear. "I won't let them hurt you." He lay down in the stall to sleep near the horse.

Early the next morning, the stable doors opened and sunlight spilled inside. Outside of Salvator's stall, Isaac heard a pair of approaching footsteps. They struck the ground ominously, heading right for the stall.

Isaac grabbed a nearby pitchfork.

The footsteps stopped right outside the stall, and the latch on the door began to creak open...

"Step back!" Isaac shouted, ready to strike the intruder.

A small Black stable boy named Henry, barely older than ten, jumped back. Isaac recognized Henry and retreated.

"Henry! You-- I thought you were--You see anybody come in here?"

"No, sir, but I just got here," Henry said, bewildered.

"Everything okay?" Henry said with worry.

Isaac realized he was still clutching the pitchfork, so he set it down.

"Listen, Henry, I don't want Salvator eating any feed the other horses aren't eating. You just make sure no one comes in here and goes anywhere near Salvator, okay?"

"Yes sir," Henry replied. "Why? You think someone wants to hurt him, Ike?

Isaac looked into the small innocent face of the stable boy.

"I don't know. Maybe I'm thinking too much," he said.

Isaac handed the boy a ten dollar bill.

"Promise me you'll look after him, Henry."

58

Isaac - 1890 - What's in that Drink?

Isaac sat with Lucy in the grandstand cafe. Lucy sensed there was something very wrong,

"You seem nervous," Lucy said.

"I am nervous," Isaac responded. "I spent time reading and praying earlier today but I am still on edge."

"Yes, way more than usual, Ike. I don't see why there's anything to be worried about," Lucy said, trying to calm him.

A waiter approached their table. "Anything to drink ma'am?"

"I'm fine, thank you," Lucy responded.

" Ginger Ale, Ike?" The waiter inquired a second time.

"Yes, thank you. Just a splash, please."

The waiter nodded and departed the table.

As the waiter prepared the Ginger Ale, he glanced across the room at Isaac and Lucy. Seeing that they were turned away, he broke open a capsule and poured it into one of the glasses. The server placed the drink in front of an unaware Isaac, smiled, and walked away.

59

Isaac - 1890 - Manmouth Racetrack

Isaac, now in his racing silks, in preparation for the race, met up once again with Henry, the stableboy.

"Anyone come near him?" Isaac inquired, worry lines surrounding his eyes.

"Only Mr. Byrnes, Ike. No one else. Made sure of that," Henry said, with certainty.

"Good work," said Isaac as he placed his cap on his head and prepared to mount Salvator.

"Alright Salvator. Let's finish our last race together strong."

As Isaac rode out onto the racetrack, he continuously rubbed his oddly bleary eyes. He reached down to pat his mother's Bible in his pocket for reassurance. The sun appeared to beat down unusually bright and hot. The cheering of the crowd seemed to enter his ear through a funnel.

He squinted. In the crowd, a woman holding a parasol shifted in and out of focus. He was feeling very dizzy. He tried to calm himself, thinking perhaps the nerves had gotten the best of him, but there was something peculiar happening. He couldn't think straight.

The horses lined up at their posts. Isaac blinked hard. The ground appeared to be inches from his face. It's as though he was living in a different dimension.

Isaac signaled to the starter that he needed more time. The starter lowered the flag. With difficulty, Isaac dismounted and adjusted his saddle. He struggled with the fastener and fell forward a bit, bracing himself against Salvator. Salvator sensed something was very wrong and whined.

The starter looked over at him, surprised at his movements and voice.

"Rider, you ready there?" the starter asked.

"Yes. Just a moment," Isaac said as he worked hard to compose himself.

Isaac breathed heavily and tried shaking himself. He adjusted in the seat once again, hoping to improve his feeling of confidence while trying to remain focused. After a moment and more confusion, he heard the starting gun blast...

But to Isaac, the blast echoed strangely in the air. Salvator took off and Isaac, unsteady, nearly lost his balance at the horse's sudden charge.

As they rode together, Isaac's field of vision blurred. The horses in front of him seemed to multiply and overlap, the track seemed to bend one way and then the other.

Trying to shake it off, Isaac slipped further and further behind the other riders. He closed his eyes coming around the far side of the track riding entirely on feeling rather than vision.

But it didn't work. Salvator, slowed to a canter as they rounded the far turn. Isaac held on tightly until he lost all sense of vision and balance. Lucy stood up in the grandstand, her mouth agape as she watched Isaac fall off of Salvator. Matt Byrnes and several stablehands ran up to Isaac and tried to help him to his feet. As Salvator was corralled by Byrnes, Isaac was carried off the track.

In the owner's section, King Kelly was standing in the center, privy to nearly every conversation and anecdote. Many spectators seemed angered. Isaac and Salvator had been heavily favored to win the race.

Among the betters on Murphy, Blackburn, confused and disgruntled, turned to King.

"What the hell happened? Murphy seemed to be completely lucid before the race?"

"Such a shame. I was afraid this would happen at some point," King observed. "What would happen?" Blackburn was startled.

"My good fellow, it is clear that Isaac Murphy was drunk on that horse. I had a private conversation with him and warned him to stop drinking the night of the match race at Sheepshead, but he no doubt has a serious problem. I mean, do you remember the clambake? He was drunk that night too."

Blackburn shook his head in disgust, "Yes. You're right. He was drinking much of the night. He's fond of champagne."

"This is outrageous," Blackburn responded. "He should be punished for this!"

"It runs in his family," King said. "His father and uncle were also drunks. Damn shame."

Isaac lay on a bench outside the lockers, ridden with sickness. Lucy sat beside him trying to attend to him. Matt Byrnes entered.

"How is he?" Matt asked.

"He's been wrenching bad. I can't wait much longer for the doctor. Where is he?" Lucy asked desperately.

"I don't know. They just suspended him, though," Byrnes said. "They just suspended Isaac for racing drunk."

"What? Why? Can't they see he's...sick? " Lucy said, choking back tears.

"They're saying he was intoxicated and they have witnesses."

Isaac riled in pain, "Jesus, Mary, and Saint Joseph.....I was poisoned!" he said while holding his stomach in agony.

"We have to get him to a hospital," Lucy pleaded, tears now streaming down her face. "And, that is a lie. I was with Isaac just before the race and all he drank was Ginger Ale."

60

Isaac - 1890 - A Fever Dream and Pain

As they lifted Isaac into the carriage en route to the hospital, Isaac's eyes flickered to the past. He was back in America's modest home in Lexington.

America sat on the bed next to young Isaac reading a book. Isaac was enraptured in America's dramatic reading of Ali Baba and the Forty Thieves.

AMERICA (reading)

"'Ill-omened woman!' exclaimed Ali Baba, 'what have you done to ruin me and my family?' 'It was to preserve, not to ruin you,' answered Marjaneh, 'for see here,' continued she, opening the false merchant's garment and showing the dagger. 'See what an enemy you have entertained! Look well at him and you will find him to be both the false oil merchant and the Captain of the gang of forty robbers.' Then Ali Baba, seeing that Marjaneh had saved his life a second time, embraced her..."

LATER...

Isaac could hear voices in the hospital room around him but the medication running through him and the poison he ingested earlier in the day seemed to be causing him to drift in and out of consciousness. He fell into a deep memory dream.

In the dream, America and Isaac were asleep in bed in their small house in Lexington when suddenly, outside, there came a whooping.

America woke up and looked out of the window.

A group of about a dozen bag-headed men were parading down the street. The men had white sheets covering their faces. Some were carrying torches, others were carrying rifles. Some of the men were yelling and screeching and banging pots and pans into the night air as they made their way through the neighborhood. America ducked down behind the window.

"What's wrong Mama?"

"I don't know, Isaac."

"Mama, I—"

"Shhh, Isaac. There's trouble out there."

"Is it robbers?"

There was a hard knock at the backdoor. America shushed Isaac and waited until…she heard a familiar voice.

"America. It's me. It's Deacon."

America still did not approach the door. She waited.

"I just want to make sure you and Isaac are alright."

Cautiously and quietly, America opened the door, relieved to see Deacon standing alone. He closed the backdoor softly behind him.

"What's going on out there, Deek?"

"I don't know but stay quiet."

America and Deacon went to the window and looked outside. Far down the street there was a commotion outside one of the houses. The bag-headed men appeared to have picked out a house down the block, cheering and taunting whoever was inside.

As America and Deacon talked to each other by the window, little Isaac went to the front door and opened it.

Isaac walked outside into the street. He stood bravely, standing guard beside the front door.

When he looked down the street he saw…further down the street…

A man with a bag over his head and two slits for eyes. A living monster. The man turned and stared directly at young Isaac.

Isaac started to tremble but he held his ground.

"Isaac!" American cried out.

America pulled young Isaac into the house...

In a hushed and furious voice Isaac heard his mother America's voice ringing in his ears. America slapped Isaac's behind—hard—something she had never done before. She caught herself before saying,

"What on God's green earth do you think you're doing boy?"

She stared daggers into him as he rubbed his backside and started to softly cry.

"Isaac Burns Murphy, you're smarter than that!" America said between gritted teeth. "Isaac, those men want to hurt you! They want to kill all of us and everyone we love."

"Shhh. They comin' this way." Deacon said softly but firmly.

America, still holding Isaac in a vice-grip, closed her eyes and prayed.

"Dear God, please let this pass away from us. Protect us Lord." America whispered a prayer.

"Meccie, they're outside."

A demon holler sounded from the street. High-pitched cackling pierced the air as the Klan tried their best to terrorize the entire Black surrounding neighborhood.

Finally, the voices faded off into the distance.

After several moments of silence, Deacon said in a whisper,

"Don't light anything for the rest of the night. Just keep quiet. Not a word."

Time passed in what seemed like an eternity of silence.

America and Isaac tried to sleep in the pitch darkness of the home as Deacon kept a tired watch over the street outside.

The hospital dream faded into a deep sleep.

61

America - 1874 - Freedman's Bank Demise

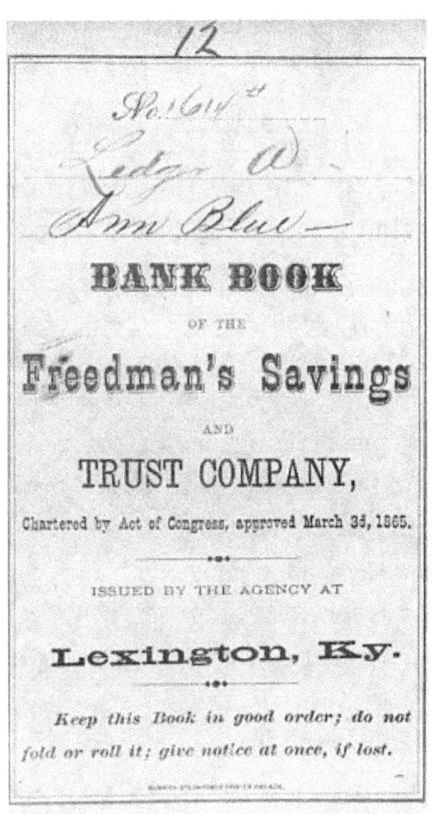

America scrubbed the floor, shaving soap into a pail of water, stirring the water, back and forth, back and forth. But where before it was routine, now it appeared cumbersome. After only a few scrubs, America had to stop and gather herself before returning.

Then she coughed, hard and harsh. Blood splattered all over the floor in front of her. America looked down at the blood splatter in horror. She took the brush in her hands and scrubbed out her own blood.

The following morning America coughed and hacked as she approached the Freedman bank building, holding Isaac's hand tightly clutched to hers. Once she was near enough, she noticed that all the windows were boarded up and the sign out in front of the bank read "Closed."

America tried to open the doors. They were all locked. The bank looked deserted. She turned to a nearby Black woman on the street.

"I don't understand what's going on with Freedman's Bank?" she asked with worry.

"It failed," the woman said.

"What failed?" America said with grave concern.

"The bank. It ain't no more," the woman said.

"What? What are you talking about?" America pleaded for an answer with sweat from fever pouring from her brow.

A man passing by tried to step in and explain.

"Bank's no more. Left me completely broke. Shouldn't have kept my money in it for as long as I did when it was going through hard times. Thought Mr. Frederick Douglass could save it, but that didn't happen."

"I don't understand," America said in a state of horror. "My money is in there. I have all my savings in that bank! All my savings! My husband's pension! Everything! Everything for my boy's future!"

"I hate to tell you ma'am, but it's gone," the man said shaking his head.

"It can't be gone! That's not—possible....Oh dear God….." her voice trailed off in sadness and desperation.

America looked at the woman and the man, and she realized that both of them had had this same conversation many times before with equally distraught people.

America walked away from the crowd, shaking mad and coughing. She told Isaac to wait as she went over to the side of the road for a moment. She staggered to the corner of the former bank building, leaned over and coughed up blood before returning to her son.

62

America - 1875 - Confrontation and Persuasion

America was working in Williams' manor, her scrubbing now laborious, sweating profusely. She kept looking up at the door, waiting...

James Williams finally entered through the front door with a stack of mail. America wiped her hands on her dress and approached him.

"Mr. Williams, sir," she said. She projected her voice as much as she was able.

Williams was sorting through the mail, not bothering to look up. After a moment, he answered without making eye contact.

"Yes, America?"

"I was wondering if I could ask you something, sir?" America said in the strongest voice she could muster.

"Alright," Williams replied.

"It's very important to me, sir."

"Alright, what is it?" Williams said casually, still not looking up.

"Will you take my boy Isaac on, as a stable hand?" America asked. There was a long pause.

"You'll have to take that up with Eli," Williams said.

"I did," America's answered back quickly.

"Eli is the one that suggested it a few years back."

Williams was paying no attention.

"I told you, sir, I did," America said again, her voice louder and stronger.

Williams finally looked up, taken aback by her directness.

"Eli said he would try but I mistakenly waited too long. I feared for my son's safety, riding and all but..." Williams cut her off.

"Right, well, you see, we have more stable boys now than we need. But I'll be sure to have Eli look into it next season. Provided he's not too old," Williams said.

"Please, sir," America continued speaking, "My boy, he's small for his age and he's a fast study. He works very hard. He would do all anyone asked of him and more."

"I understand, America," Williams countered. "We like good workers. And you have done a fine job here in the house. Remind Eli next season and maybe he'll have an opening," Williams said, clearly intending to close the conversation.

"Eli said he would try to help when I asked him again yesterday..." America's voice cracked as she continued speaking.

"I understand. I..." Williams said.

America stood firm with the last bit of strength she had in her and took a step towards Williams.

"No, you don't understand, sir." America looked him directly in the eyes.

America's reproach startled him.

"I'm very sick, Mr. Williams. I don't know if I have much more time left on earth and the Freedman Bank has completely failed us... I've worked all of my life to make a better way for my son, Isaac. All I'm asking for is a chance."

Williams didn't know how to respond. He stood there with a mix of embarrassment and admiration.

"Oh, I see. How old is he?" Williams inquired.

"He's fourteen now. But he looks at least four years younger. Jordan says he will be a great rider."

"Oh, no, that's too old to get started," Williams said as he turned away.

"I know but he's fast and strong. He's smart. He will work to be the best," America said matter-of-factly.

There was a long pause before Williams' responded, finally with a sense of slight compassion, "Fine."

"You'll bring him on then?" America asked again with hope.

"Why not?" Williams finally relented.

"Oh thank you very much, sir. I thank you very much," America said with relief. She turned away, grateful her efforts had finally succeeded.

There was a pause.

"And America..." Williams said as he turned to face her.

"Yes, sir," America said obediently.

Williams seemed prepared to reprimand her for her insubordination. But when he looked at her again, he suddenly seemed intimidated at the prospect.

"The lamps. The lamps in Masie's room. I'd like those polished before she returns home."

"Yes, sir. Thank you, sir," America said as she curtsied and walked away.

63

America - 1875 - Williams' Stables, Morning

Young Isaac was accompanied by his mother America, as they approached Williams' stable. Waiting for them outside the barn doors was a smiling Eli Jordan. He approached them, looking eager and excited to greet his new pupil.

"Hi, Uncle Eli," Isaac said, beaming.

"Hello, Isaac. I am so happy to see you here today!" Eli said. "I have been waiting and hoping for this day for a long time."

From that day forward, Uncle Eli began teaching Isaac about how to take care of a stable and its inhabitants, the Thoroughbred horses that lived there. Eli had a unique way of teaching his stable boys, with tough love and discipline. He included important lessons that would stay with them for life.

One of his lessons was about speed and accuracy.

"Have you ever paid attention to your Mama while she's workin'?" He asked Isaac one day. "When she cleans a room, she cleans it with perfection. She don't sweep dust into a corner thinkin' nobody will see it there. She is only interested in doin' it right. Now I want you to think about your Mama's way of doin' things while you clean out the stable stalls. It don't matter if it's horses instead of people, you gotta begin doin' everything with her habits in mind. And every stall you clean you count out loud, markin' the time. And as you get better and better at it, you keep markin' the time, trying to do it faster but still do it perfect."

Eli continued, "The man that succeeds does it better than anybody else in less time. That's the same whether it's cuttin' hair as a barber or runnin' in a horserace. Cause if he's a barber and he does it faster, he can do twice as many in the time it takes someone else to do one. Time is money, especially on the racetrack, where your time difference is the difference 'tween winnin' and losin'".

Another lesson Eli talked about was getting in the right mindset mentally to ride a horse to victory.

"Now when you're feeling down or upset about somethin', go off and pound your fists in the dirt, but don't bring that feelin' to the horse," he told Isaac. "Cause that horse can feel your anger, your nerves and everythin' else when you're ridin' it. It's a living thing, just like you. Just cause it don't talk the way we do, doesn't mean it can't hear you. So be kind to it, try to be calm and take away its fears, don't add to them. You gotta both be thinking positive things and workin' together to make a team. The horse likes to run and likes to win, but it don't like being whipped and beaten. So encourage it to do what it was born to do. Don't ever punish it like a slave driver. That horse is not your slave, he is your friend, so treat him like one."

Eli knew how to train horses and how to teach stable boys to become great jockeys. He knew how to push the horse just enough to cross the finish line at maximum speed to win but no further. He was a great judge of pacing. He taught Isaac how to study the horse's moods, and how to hold back and speed up and where to navigate on the track in and out of other riders depending on their position on the rail. He taught Isaac how to do his homework when it came to understanding the moves of other riders and horses Isaac was competing with. Eli was a genius when it came to Thoroughbred horse racing, but more importantly, he was a great judge of character. And he took special care of Isaac who was the perfect student.

64

Isaac - 1891 - A Special Visitor with News

Anthony Hamilton

Photo credit: Keeneland Library Hemment Collection

After the incident at Manmouth Park and his grave illness as a result of being drugged, Isaac rallied to win his third Kentucky Derby in grand style in 1891, riding a Thoroughbred named Kingman. Kingman was the first horse in American history that was co-owned by an

African American, a horse trainer named Dudley Allen. Dudley had also been the son of slaves in Kentucky.

After his historic win on Kingman at Churchill Downs, Isaac was presented with a "golden purse" and praised from coast to coast and around the world in the press.

But those who sought to destroy his reputation and legacy continued to spread rumors about his drinking. Caricature artist illustrators began publishing hideous cartoons of Black jockeys and there was intense pressure to persuade wealthy horse owners to give their top mounts to White immigrant jockeys in the North.

Racial tensions were growing to a fever pitch and incidents of foul play and abuse to horses mounted by Black jockeys was also growing.

There was little that Isaac could do to prevent the hate that was taking over the sport of horse racing in America. Black riders were beginning to speak among themselves about leaving the U.S. for Europe, where they hoped to get fair treatment and compensation for their victories at the racetrack. And as all of this was unfolding, Isaac's nagging illness continued and during the latter weeks in 1891, left him bedridden.

During an extended period of ill health, Isaac lay in bed, as Lucy sat beside him, reading aloud:

"They are not green like the pines, nor gray like the stones, nor blue like the sky; but they have, to my eyes, if possible, yet rarer colors, like flowers and precious stones, as if they were the pearls or crystals of the Walden water. I never chanced--"

"Lucy?"

Lucy turned at the sound of a familiar voice behind her. Anthony Hamilton had entered the room. Lucy quickly closed the book she was reading and rushed toward him, embracing Tony in a giant bear hug.

"Tony! I thought you were in California?" Lucy exclaimed with excitement.

"I came back as fast as I could. I wanted to see you two," Tony replied warmly.

Isaac looked up to see his best friend and childhood rival and managed to get out a few words. "Come back later. I'm nappin'!"

Tony could tell that Isaac was awake and despite his frail condition, still had a sense of humor. He decided to play along.

"Beauty sleep huh? You sure could use it," Tony teased with a shrug.

Isaac wheezed out a laugh. Then Tony made an announcement.

"I have some big news I wanted to share with you and Lucy, Ike. Annie and me—we're doing it. We're getting married. I asked her and she said 'Yes'!"

"Oh, Tony! That's wonderful!" Lucy said gleefully.

"Annie has no idea what she's in for," Isaac said as he rolled over with a big smile on his face.

Tony continued, "Guess what, Ike, you better get better quick, 'cause I want you to be my best man!"

"So are you finally admitting I am the best man after all?"

"I guess I am, but only when you are standing at the aisle next to me while I get hitched."

65

Isaac - 1891 - A Young Admirer

More days passed, and Isaac was trying hard to regain his strength.

There was a knock at the door. Lucy answered it, greeting a small, shy White girl named Nannie Atchinson—eight years old—holding a fresh basket of fruit.

"Good morning, Nannie! Oh my, those look delicious," Lucy said gratefully as she took the basket from Nannie and paid her with a handful of coins.

Nannie looked up at her.

"Mrs. Murphy?"

"Yes, hon'?"

"I made something for Isaac. I was wondering if you could give it to him?"

Nannie handed Lucy a small clay sculpture of a horse—crude but made with great care.

"I love Isaac," Nannie said, her eyes twinkling with admiration.

"I went with my Pa, and I saw him ride last summer. I tried hard to make the horse look like the one I saw Isaac ride then. I know I'm a girl, but I want to ride and be a jockey someday too. I have big dreams."

Lucy bent down and looked directly into Nannie's eyes—eyes filled with innocence, wonder, and hope for the future.

"That's wonderful. Say, I think if your Pa says it's okay, maybe someday soon we can take you to our stables and get you up on one of Isaac's real horses. I know Isaac would enjoy that."

Nannie was overjoyed with excitement. "That would be a dream come true!"

66

Isaac - 1891 - The Big Party for a Best Friend

Lucy helped Isaac walk slowly through the parlor. He struggled a bit, leaning on her for support.

"Feeling better it seems," Lucy observed.

"How many bottles of champagne do we have?" Isaac asked.

"What?" Lucy replied, surprised by the question.

Isaac smiled broadly, "We're going to need to buy out the town."

He looked back at Lucy's confused and worried expression.

"I have an idea, Lucy," Isaac said. "It might be my best idea ever."

"Really, Ike? Because you've had some real winners and this one sounds like one of those," Lucy said, rolling her eyes.

Isaac, though still weak, seemed joyful. "We're going to throw a great big party, Luc."

Lucy looked puzzled, "Your fever dreams must be getting worse."

"No, listen," Isaac continued. "An engagement party for Tony and Annie. We will put it on right here in our home."

"Invite everyone, rich and poor. Make it the occasion of the year," Isaac said, his eyes lighting up.

Lucy's hands went to her hips. "Isaac, you're still barely able to move." She shook her head but smiled faintly.

"My dancing might be hindered some but that shouldn't discourage the others," Isaac said, sounding more like himself again. "Tony deserves it and I want to do this for him."

67

Isaac - 1891 - An Engagement Party for the Ages

Throughout the Murphy mansion, tables were set, flowers and ornate decorations had been perfectly placed. Isaac, now using a cane, smiled as he watched caterers and house workers transform the Murphy mansion into an occasion for a grand celebration.

Night time approached. A carriage pulled up in front of the mansion. Tony and his fiancé Annie—a beautiful young woman in her twenties—disembarked and looked up in amazement at the illuminated Murphy mansion.

Inside, Tony and Annie enjoyed the warmth of family and friends at what would become known as the most extravagant and welcoming party Lexington had ever seen.

As the festivities continued throughout the mansion, Isaac stood out on the observation tower next to his childhood best friend, Anthony Hamilton. The rival duo—the two greatest Black jockeys in America—looked out over the silent racetrack in the distance.

After a few moments silence, Anthony spoke first.

"Never thought we'd get here. Did you Ike?"

"I was certain of it," Isaac replied quickly and confidently.

"Really? With all the odds stacked against us?" Anthony laughed, only to catch the unmovable expression on his friend's face. There was no doubt that Isaac truly believed it.

Another long pause followed.

Then they began teasing each other again, just like old times.

"Well, you do know who ruined your perfect record of four in a row at the American Derby in Chicago in 1887, right?" Anthony said, puffing his chest out.

Isaac snapped back, "Well, I came back and beat you in that same race in 1888 to make four American Derby wins— I won my third Kentucky Derby just a few months ago on Kingman." Isaac grinned. "How many golden purses you got on display at Churchill Downs for mounting the first Thoroughbred in history to be co-owned by a colored man named Dudley Allen?"

Not to be outdone, Anthony countered again.

"You know the last race we ran—you know who came out on top, right?"

"Queen's Handicap?" Isaac asked knowingly.

"It was you who always used to say the last one's the only one that counts."

"I guess that makes me better, huh?" Anthony said matter-of-factly.

"Oh, but that won't be the last one, Tony," Isaac said, puffing his chest out proudly.

"Are you kiddin' me, brother? You're coming back?" Tony asked, disbelief in his voice.

"Of course I'm coming back," Isaac stated proudly. "I'm building up my stable like Dudley did, riding under my own colors, hiring my own trainers."

"You always had ambition, Ike. You always worked to be the best. I'll give you that,"Anthony said, looking out at the track.

"The track wouldn't ever be the same without you, Ike."

Down on the lawn, several guests had begun to gather.

Anthony noticed the group and looked down in surprise.

"What in the... what is everybody doing outside in this cold? I thought we were the only ones that were crazy standing out here," he said.

Lucy and Annie appeared from behind, joining Anthony and Isaac on the observation tower.

"Before what's about to happen next, I want you to know—I moved the horses from the stables over there. Didn't want to scare them," Isaac said with a wink.

"Scare them? Ike, what are you talking about?" Anthony asked, puzzled.

Just then, a whistling sound erupted from the racetrack—followed by a loud BANG!

Anthony and Annie watched in amazement as fireworks exploded over the racetrack grounds. The party-goers on the lawn cheered as bright lights blasted across the night sky. This was a spectacle none of them had ever seen before.

Isaac and Lucy retreated quietly to give Anthony and Annie space to enjoy the moment.

Sitting together at the top of the tower steps, Isaac and Lucy gazed into each other's eyes lovingly—just as they had long ago at the Craw Bottom dancehall. It was indeed, a happy night.

68

Isaac - 1891 - Forgiveness

Isaac and Lucy rode in their carriage through the streets of Lexington.

"I must say you're looking much more lively. The party did you good," Lucy remarked.

"I'm itching to get back on the track," Isaac said, leaning into Lucy as the carriage rattled along the brick road. "By the way, you're going to have to help me think of a name for the stables—and the racing colors too."

"Pink," Lucy said quickly.

"Pink?" Isaac questioned, raising an eyebrow.

Suddenly, without warning, Isaac spotted a Black man running into the street.

The carriage swerved abruptly, as the driver struggled to reign in the horse, skidding dangerously to a stop.

The driver yelled at the man who darted into the road, "What in the hell is wrong with you?"

Isaac winced as he leaped out of the carriage and ran over to the man, thinking he might be hurt.

"Forgive me! Please, Mr. Isaac Murphy! Forgive me," the man pleaded.

Recognition crossed Isaac's face. It was the man he had met at Haggin's mansion— the one he thought was his Uncle Charlie who had disappeared into the night.

"I'm sorry. I'm sorry," the man stammered, struggling through his drunken state to get the words out.

"It's okay. Straighten yourself out, man. What's wrong with you?" Isaac said as he tried to make sense of the situation.

"I been tryin' to find you. I—I didn't have no money. They offered me money and I— I'm barely getting by as is. I didn't want to have to do it. I'm sorry!"

"What is it? Come out with it!" Isaac demanded.

"I ain't your uncle," the man blurted out.

"You what?" Isaac said, anger rising in his voice.

"I had to say those things. I'm sorry! I didn't know your father, I..."
Isaac grabbed the man by the lapels, fuming.

"Who are you!?!" Isaac shouted, getting close to the man's face.

"My name is ...." the man stammered, his voice cracking.

"What kind of game are you playing?" Isaac said, furious.

"My name is Tobias!" the man said through his tears.

Isaac let go of him and watched him stumble to the ground.

"You run out in the middle of the street like that in front of a horse and carriage? You could have seriously injured us! Scare a horse like that and you could have killed yourself!"

"I'm sorry. I just—I needed you to know," Tobias said, choking on the words.

"Who put you up to this?" Isaac demanded.

"There were several of 'em. A man with bushy chops and grey streaks in his hair. Another who was bald. And another man-- there was the man with a gold ring. A big one. Said his name was Baker. I—They'll kill me if they heard I told you. But I had to. I couldn't live with myself," Tobias said, his voice filled with shame.

"I hope they paid you well," Isaac remarked bitterly.

Isaac coughed and winced, turning away from the deceitful Tobias, who was now crying in the middle of the street. But just as Isaac was about to climb back into the carriage, he stopped himself.

Tobias cowered as Isaac stepped toward him—but instead of lashing out, the jockey reached down and helped him to his feet.

"Here," Isaac said with compassion. He pulled out several bills of money and handed them to the man. "Go on."

"Bless you Mister Murphy. Bless you," Tobias called after him.

Isaac, saddened, walked back and returned to his carriage.

69

Isaac - 1896 - Vivid Memories

Isaac prepared for the next few seasons, but it was clear that he was still battling nagging illness and weakness.

Wearing his new pink and blue racing silks, Isaac winced as he rode down the track during a race. Ahead of him, two White jockeys—one Italian and the other Irish— worked in tandem, deliberately blocking his advancement. They boxed him out skillfully, exchanging sinister smiles as they collaborated to disadvantage him. After the race, Isaac tucked away his racing clothes in a satchel, but suddenly doubled over, grabbing his stomach in pain. He tried to stand but eventually collapsed to the ground.

A crowd gathered as Isaac was carried into the hospital on a stretcher.

Outside of a hospital room, Lucy spoke with a White doctor. After a brief, grim exchange, the doctor walked away, leaving her standing in the hallway with her head in her hands. Time passed and Lucy paced back and forth. Finally, she sat at Isaac's bedside, reading to him from his favorite books and from his mother America's Bible.

Eventually, Lucy drifted off to sleep on the couch beside him.

Isaac stirred. Struggling to keep his eyes open, he flickered in and out of consciousness, slipping once again into...a dream of the past.

He saw himself at the Williams' stables early in the morning. Waiting for him in the distance was Eli Jordan.

"So what do you say, Isaac? Ready to get to work?" Eli Jordan's voice was firm and clear.

America stood beside him, patting her son's head and giving him a gentle push forward.

"Yes, he is. He's going to be the best," she said warmly.

He heard Eli's calm voice continue:

"You know, Isaac, horses can sense much more than you'd realize. A horse knows what you're thinking—what you're feelin'."

Isaac drifted in and out of consciousness again but the dream continued...

He saw himself pitching hay into a stall, stopping to admire the horse inside as Eli's voice echoed in his ears:

"A horse takes on the temperament of the one that trains it. If you're cruel, that horse'll be cruel. If you're kind, that horse'll be kind."

Young Isaac approached the horse nervously, reaching out a hand.

"It all starts with respect. You got to respect them— and most importantly, they gotta respect you," Eli said.

Later, Isaac saw himself reach out to touch the horse, Volcano, who responded by gently turning its head toward him.

Isaac saw himself curled up on a straw mattress in the stable. Though several other stable boys were sleeping on mounds of hay nearby, he alone was awake, staring up through the slats in the roof at the twinkling night sky, still hearing Eli's steady voice:

"Once you build that bond—once the reins become part of your hands and the hooves beat along with the sound of your blood—you both become more than you were. You become something new, together."

In the vision, he saw that Eli was waiting for his fourteen-year-old self to approach the large black stallion named Volcano.

"Okay, Let's see what you got, Isaac. Time to mount," Eli encouraged.

Isaac backed away nervously.

"I don't know how to do this," he said fearfully.

"Good," Eli answered. "Learnin' starts with not knowin' a thing. Go on now…"

Isaac was hoisted up to the stirrup but struggled to maintain his balance. After shifting and wobbling, he finally swung himself into the saddle.

As soon as he was mounted, Volcano jolted. Frightened, Isaac tugged back on the reins.

The horse bucked.

Isaac lost his grip.

The small boy was thrown hard into the dirt. He flailed, trying to scramble away from the frenetic hooves of the wild horse above him.

Finally, he managed to roll out of harm's way.

"Woah! Steady!" Isaac heard Eli's soothing voice again.

Eli worked to calm the aggravated horse and went over to Isaac. Lifting the boy's chin, he saw tears streaming down Isaac's face.

"I told you, Uncle Eli, I can't! I can't do it!" Isaac cried.

"You really believe that?" Eli asked quietly. "What are you more afraid of—Volcano or yourself?" Eli asked.

After a moment, Isaac answered, "Volcano."

Eli smiled.

"Well, the name don't help much. I'll give you that. But look at me. You're pullin' his head back and he don't like that. You've got to give him some slack. Relax. He's sensing your fear."

Young Isaac, tears still clouding his eyes, listened carefully.

"Don't be scared of what you don't know. Be scared of not having the courage to understand it. Try again," Eli said firmly.

Isaac hesitated.

"He's going to kill me. I can't," he said.

"Come on and get up," Eli said, tough but caring. He yanked Isaac up by the collar.

"You come from fightin' stuff! It's in your blood! Don't ever come around here saying you can't! You got to go on anyhow! Get up!"

Isaac, angry, wrestled himself away from Eli's grasp.

"There it is. Use that! Use that emotion!" Eli shouted encouragingly.

Waking from the fever dream, Isaac heard faint voices above him in the hospital bed. He tried to open his eyes but drifted back into sleep.

The dream continued.

He saw himself working in the stables, riding and improving. He observed himself waking up early and working late, sleeping on the hay in the barn.

He saw himself whispering Shakespeare's sonnets and Bible verses into horse's ears.

He grew stronger.

He saw an older version of himself, now eighteen, sitting on a fence post, watching a horse gallup across a pasture as he laced up his boots.

He saw himself reading a book, practicing with Tony and the other jockeys at the stable.

Eli Jordan's voice came back to him— talking about Isaac's first major Stakes race at Saratoga coming up that August of 1879.

He saw a playbill announcing his name in the race and the size of the purse in a newspaper.

Then, in the dream, a distraught messenger ran up to him. The messenger said something very upsetting to him. Isaac looked up alarmed.

He saw himself sprinting across the platform of a train station—then racing through the streets of Lexington on horseback, as though his life depended on it.

He arrived at America's small house, his former childhood home. He quickly dismounted, his hands shaking as he quickly tied the horse to a post.

He flew up the front stoop—no time to knock—and barged into the house.

Once inside, he rushed towards the back of the room.

James stood at the threshold.

"Isaac! You made it back," James said with relief.

Cora's head peeked out from behind a curtain.

"Isaac's here!" she said excitedly.

Isaac rushed to the bed where America lay, her eyes closed, her breathing slow. Her small Bible was clutched in her hands atop the sheet.

When she sensed him nearby, she loosened her grip and the Bible fell onto the bed beside her.

Jenny—now in her early thirties—the young girl who America had taught to read and write at the Tanner farm and who was present at Isaac's birth, was seated next to the bed. She rose from her chair, hugged Isaac, and helped him sit down.

Isaac looked at his mother lying there, close to death. She seemed too weak to speak but she looked at him, knowing he was there right beside her.

"Mama, I will be racing in my first big Stakes race at Saratoga this weekend—you will be racing with me," Isaac said in a warm, strong voice.

When she heard her son's words, America turned her head slightly towards him, letting him know she understood.

Isaac looked in his mother's eyes, seeing them widen.

"Mama, I'm ready to make you proud and be the best. I will be able to make a good living from now on. You don't have to worry about me. Uncle Eli said I have been his best pupil— and he is mounting me on his best horse, a champion horse named Falsetto," Isaac said, trying to stay strong for his mother.

He squeezed her hand gently and said firmly to her.

"Mama, I ride to win and I will be riding for you."

His words registered. America closed her eyes and squeezed his hand back in response.

Tears fell from Isaac's face on the wooden floor that night as he sat holding his mother's hand in one, and her Bible in the other as she peacefully passed away.

70

Isaac - 1896 - The End is Near

Isaac was lying in his bed again, emaciated. His breathing was shallow. He was staring out the window, as tears formed at the edges of his eyes.

In the corner of the room sat Anthony and Annie. Lucy and the attending doctor were hovering by the door. As Lucy tried to control her crying, down the hall, Eli Jordan appeared.

Lucy wrapped herself around the old horse trainer as he entered. He stood there solemn and stone-faced. He hugged Lucy back.

"He waited for you, Uncle Eli," Lucy said.

After they separated, Eli made his way to Isaac's bed. He placed his hands on Isaac's thin shoulders and leaned over to speak to him. America's Bible sat on the table beside him.

Eli glanced over and saw the Bible there, and his eyes moved back over to Isaac.

"My boy," Eli said in a comforting voice. "You have made your mother and all of us so proud."

Isaac blinked, a hint of a smile crossed his lips as a tear rolled down the side of his face. He looked up at Eli and back to his mother's Bible. His breathing became more shallow until...Isaac breathed his last.

71

Isaac - 1896 - A Funeral for a Prince

Days passed. Black curtains were draped over mirrors. Trophies and flowers were displayed throughout the various rooms. A large group of mourners dressed in black milled about the inside of the Murphy Mansion.

In front of a set of bay windows, a copper casket with silver trimmings stood. Several people approached the casket and set flowering bouquets on either side.

Lucy was approached by mourners, as she shook their hands and listened to their condolences, she noticed... peeking through a window, hands against the glass, the small, sad face of twelve-year-old Nannie Atchinson. Since her first visit in 1891, Nannie and Isaac had spent time together and Isaac had taught the young girl to ride confidently, using many of the lessons taught to him by Eli. The two had developed a very special bond. During some of his toughest days of illness and discouragement, the joy Nannie brought to Isaac's life had been a refuge.

Lucy politely excused herself from the well-wishers and went to the window. She waved for Nannie to come inside.

The pallbearers lifted Isaac's casket and carried it toward the door of his home in a procession. Lucy, wearing a black dress, followed di-

188

rectly behind with Nannie beside her. As she made it to the door she looked outside to see...hundreds of people gathered on the street to pay homage to the great jockey. There were so many mourners, they stretched in a line as far as the eye could see.

Lucy was awestruck, searching through the faces of the crowd, mostly Black folks, but a good number of White people as well, and a mix of young, old and everything in between. There were young stable boys, fans, newsmen, politicians, the richest and poorest folks from Lexington and everything in between. Some had traveled in from out of town and far away. There were even White wealthy turf men in attendance, mixed in with the crowd of local mourners. Standing at the front of the crowd were Tony and Annie, Sarah, Cora, Jenny, Deacon, James and the Jordan family.

The hearse made its way to African Cemetery No. 2 in Lexington. Pallbearers lowered Isaac's casket into the ground as the preacher opened America's small Bible and began reciting prayers. When he was finished, he handed the Bible back to Lucy.

As the mourners left the cemetery, Lucy hugged Nannie, Annie, Tony and the entire Jordan family. She paused in front of the wooden grave marker of America Murphy, now lying in the African Cemetery No. 2 plot next to her son.

72

America - 1879 - African Cemetery No. 2

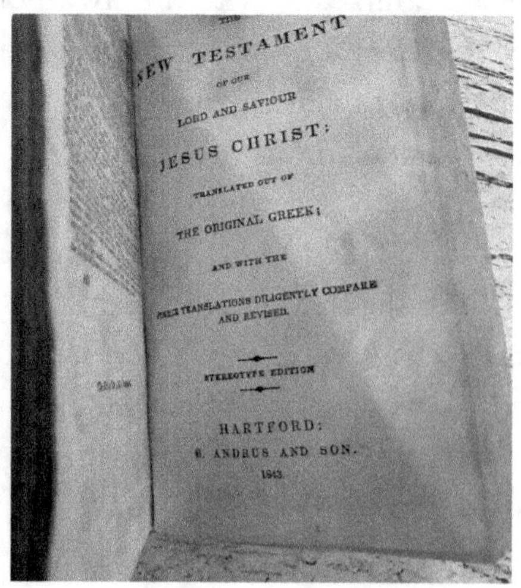

An eighteen-year-old Isaac stood in the exact same spot before the gravesite of his mother, watching as those who knew her including Sarah, Jenny, Cora, Deacon, James and the Jordans passed by, casting dirt and seashells.

Dusk was folding over the sky but Isaac remained, standing in the same spot, still looking down at a grave holding his mother's precious Bible.

In the silence of the house that evening, Isaac sat by the window thinking. He paused to open the Bible to read a few passages, trying to process his mother's death. At the age eighteen, he was now a fully grown man. He had trained hard and long for four years with Eli and was now facing the biggest race of his life. This would be a Stakes race in New York with a winning purse that had the potential to secure his financial future.

Deacon sat nearby while Cora was busy folding blankets. She looked over at him.

"You sure you don't need anything, Ike?" Cora asked.

"I didn't pack anything. I didn't bring any other clothes. I left them out East," Isaac said. "I was trying to get here as fast as I could. All I brought were the clothes on my back."

"You're racing in that big Stakes race at Saratoga this weekend, right?" Cora inquired.

"That was the plan, but now I don't know," Isaac said sadly.

"You do what you have to do, boy. Ain't no worry with you stayin' here. We can take care of everything. You just stay as long as you like, honey."

Deacon chimed in, "Might do you good to get moving. Get blood flowing in a certain direction, Isaac. That's what your Mama would want."

"I suppose you're right," Isaac said.

"She loved to see you race. She'd get so nervous, it was like she was right there in the saddle with you. If she were here now she'd be saying, something like..."

"I know, I know," Isaac picked up on Deacon's thought, impersonating his mother, "You mopin'? Come on now, don't cry over me. Get moving. Come on now, you've got a race! You gonna be the best?"

Deacon laughed. "Well...? I guess that settles it, don't it? Let's get you on the next train out."

73

America - 1879 - Saturday at Saratoga

Saratoga Grandstand

Photo credit: Keeneland Library Hemment Collection

In his racing silks at dawn, Isaac approached the horse he would be riding, Falsetto.

He walked up to the steed carefully and cautiously, as though it were a baby sleeping in a crib. He removed his hat, and brushed the mane, smoothing out the fur around the muzzle. The horse seemed to understand him, it seemed to speak to him without words.

Isaac road Falsetto out onto the track in the early morning for practice. Even though the training track was empty, Isaac could visualize the stands buzzing with excitement and energy as in his mind, he saw the horses and jockeys making their way to their post positions. He saw the crowd in the distance.

Isaac was somber as he sat in the saddle, his thoughts not on the race but back with his mother.

And then he heard...

"Isaac!" Jenny was running out into the sunlight after him with excitement. She was calling his name just as she had done the day he was born.

There, standing at the rail on the far end of the training track, Isaac saw a small group of friends and distant relatives. Standing with Jenny were Deacon, James, Cora and Sarah, those who had been at America's side at the very beginning of his life on the Tanner farm. He also saw the Jordan girls, Emily, Lydia and Lily Jordan waving bonnets in the breeze.

"We had to be here, Isaac! We wanted to see you ride! We got enough money to get on the all-night train so we could be here all together," Jenny shouted gleefully.

Isaac smiled broadly. He took in the sight of this small crowd standing on the rail, many of them former slaves, a family of true beauty. They had traveled all this way to support him.

His face brightened. He waved and nodded.

And then he saw her...

Standing further out along the rail, watching him, was his mother, America. It must have been an apparition, but Isaac could see her clearly all the same. She smiled and mouthed a single word:

"Go."

Isaac lined up at the starting line of the training track. There was a new sense of composure—a new rush of adrenaline entering his body.

Something new and different and wild filled his spirit. His eyes focused on the track, his heart rate slowed, and the only sound he could hear was the horse beneath him breathing.

He said to himself and the apparition.

"Mama, I'm ready."

Isaac was on the track in the middle of the race with Falsetto against Spendthrift at Saratoga. And the sound of the starting gun was not a jolt, but a drum commencing a natural thrust of movement. Like dancers, Isaac and his horse were leaping from the line...

The rest was inevitable, even as the other horses surrounded him, even as the early riders rushed past him.....

Isaac remained focused. He knew that his time had come, he knew that if he waited, if he rode it out with all he had learned, with all he had become with Eli's training...and with his mother's inspiration, he would succeed.

A clearing presented itself in front of him as the horses rounded the stretch in the race at Saratoga. Horse and rider surged forward...

And with the reins in his hands, Isaac crossed the finish line and waved at the crowd cheering in the distance. The Winner.

Isaac Burns Murphy is estimated to have won 44% of the Thoroughbred horse races he competed in, a feat that remains unmatched in racing history.

He is considered by many to be the greatest jockey who ever lived.

THE END

Isaac Burns Murphy

Photo credit: Keeneland Library Hemment Collection

Definitions and Historical Information

From Wikipedia, the free encyclopedia and AI generated historical information and other sources noted below.

The American Civil War (April 12, 1861 – May 26, 1865) was the Civil War in the United States between the Union ("the North") and the Confederacy ("the South"), which was formed in 1861 by states that had seceded from the Union. The central conflict leading to war was a dispute over whether slavery should be permitted to expand into the western territories, leading to more slave states, or be prohibited from doing so, which many believed would place slavery on a course of ultimate extinction.

Decades of controversy over slavery came to a head when Abraham Lincoln, who opposed slavery's expansion, won the 1860 U.S. Presidential election. By the end of the war, much of the South's infrastructure was destroyed. The Confederacy collapsed, slavery was abolished, and four million enslaved Black people were freed. The war-torn nation then entered the Reconstruction era in an attempt to rebuild the country, bring the former Confederate states back into the United States, and grant civil rights to freed slaves.

Kentucky in the American Civil War was a Southern border state of key importance during the conflict. It officially declared its neutrality at the beginning of the war, but after a failed attempt by Confederate General Leonidas Polk to take the state of Kentucky for the Confederacy, the legislature petitioned the Union Army for assistance.

The Confederacy controlled more than half of Kentucky early in the war. Within the state, slaves were held on plantations by landowners who supported the Confederacy. In the historiography of the United States, Kentucky is primarily regarded as a Southern border state characterized by social divisions during the secession crisis, invasions, raids, internal violence, sporadic guerrilla warfare, federal-state relations, the end of slavery and the return of Confederate veterans.

From the National Archives: The Emancipation Proclamation

President Abraham Lincoln issued the Emancipation Proclamation as the nation approached its third year of bloody civil war. The proclamation declared that "all persons held as slaves within the rebellious states are, and henceforward shall be free." It applied only to states that had seceded from the United States, leaving slavery untouched in the border states. Most importantly, the freedom it promised depended upon the Union (United States) military victory.

Although the Emancipation Proclamation did not end slavery throughout the nation, it captured the hearts and imagination of millions of Americans and fundamentally transformed the character of the war. Moreover, the Proclamation announced the acceptance of Black men into the Union Army and Navy, enabling those who were liberated to become liberators themselves.

By the war's end, almost 200,000 Black soldiers and sailors had fought for the Union and for freedom. From the earliest days of the Civil War, enslaved people acted to secure their own liberty. As a milestone on the road to slavery's final destruction, the Emancipation Proclamation has assumed a prominent place among the great documents of human freedom.

Isaac Burns Murphy (January 6, 1861 – February 16, 1896) was an American Hall of Fame jockey, considered to be one of the greatest riders in American Thoroughbred horse racing history. He was the first jockey to be inducted into the National Museum of Racing and Hall of Fame at its creation in 1955.

Isaac was born into slavery on January 6, 1861, in Clark County, Kentucky. His mother, America Murphy, worked as a house slave on the Pleasant Green farm owned by David Tanner until the fall of 1864 when records indicate that she became a refugee at the Union Army depot at Camp Nelson.

Isaac's father, Jerry Burns, escaped from bondage and enlisted in the 114th U.S. Colored Troops at Camp Nelson in the summer of 1864. Jerry died at a Confederate prisoner-of-war camp in 1865 after fighting in several major battles.

After the war ended, America and Isaac moved in with family friend Eli Jordan, a man who would become one of the most important figures in Isaac's life. Eli was a prominent horse trainer working for the Williams and Owings stables and, according to historian Pellom McDaniels III: "Isaac may have been the son Eli never had, and he impressed on the boy his definition of manhood, the importance of prudence and honesty, and the benefits of being consistent in all things."

Murphy began his racing career riding for Williams and Owings stables in 1875 at the age of 14. What followed was one of the most illustrious careers in the history of the sport, during which Murphy became one of the highest-paid athletes and among the most famous Black men in America.

Murphy rode in eleven Kentucky Derbies, winning three times: on Buchanan in 1884, Riley in 1890, and Kingman in 1891.

Kingman was owned by Jacobin Stables (co-owners Preston Kinzea Stone and Dudley Allen) and trained by Dudley Allen, making it the first horse co-owned by an African-American to win the Kentucky Derby. Murphy is the only jockey to have won the Kentucky Derby, the Kentucky Oaks, and the Clark Handicap in the same year (1884). That same year, he also won the very first American Derby at Washington Park in Chicago, which was the most prestigious and highest paying "purse" in horse racing at that time.

Among the most famous races of Murphy's career was a match race at Sheepshead Bay on June 25, 1890. At the height of his career, Murphy rode Salvator to a dead-heat victory over Tenny and his rival jockey, Edward "Snapper" Garrison. The race was considered one of the most thrilling races of all time, featuring a head-to-head match up between the most dominant Black jockey squared off against the most dominant White jockey. The race is also notable for being credited with the first instance of a "photo-finish," captured by photographer John C. Hemment.

According to his own calculations, Murphy won 628 of his 1,412 starts—a 44% victory rate that has never been equaled. Hall of Fame jockey Eddie Arcaro remarked: "There is no chance that his record of winning will ever be surpassed."

America Murphy Burns (1840 - August 1879) was born into slavery. Her father, Green Murphy, who was also enslaved, was a bell ringer, auction crier and a horseman well known in the Lexington area. She was an accomplished laundress on the Pleasant Green Farm and provided laundry and housekeeping services for many families after the Civil War while raising her only son, Isaac Burns Murphy, who was highly intelligent and literate.

At age 14, America apprenticed Isaac to Eli Jordan, a prominent horse trainer who had been a family friend of her father's. There is a plaque recognizing America Murphy Burns in African Cemetery No. 2 in Lexington where her name appears along with the names of her son Isaac, Isaac's wife, Lucy Carr Murphy, and Lucy's mother, Susan Osborn.

"Jumping the Broom"

During slavery in the United States, Black couples were not allowed to legally marry. Jumping the broom emerged as a way for them to publicly declare their commitment in the absence of a legal or religious marriage. America likely "married" Jerry Burns in this fashion. She conceived a son with Jerry, Isaac Burns Murphy.

Jerry Burns was the biological father of Isaac Burns Murphy. Jerry escaped from the Skilling Farm in 1864 and joined the Union Army by enlisting in the United States Colored Troops 114th Division at Camp Nelson, near Lexington. Jerry died during the war before being reunited with his wife and son. Jerry is also listed as Jerry Skilling in some U.S. Army historical war records.

United States Colored Troops (USCT) were Union Army regiments during the American Civil War primarily composed of African Americans. The courage displayed by colored troops during the Civil

War played an important role in African Americans gaining new rights.

Camp Nelson Refugee Expulsion

Beginning in 1864, thousands of Black men, women and children escaped slavery and journeyed to Camp Nelson. While enlisting in the U.S. Army provided a clear path to emancipation for eligible men, any enslaved person from Kentucky who arrived at Camp Nelson but was unable to serve in the Army was expected to leave the camp and return to enslavement. This solution was neither feasible nor desired by the freedom seekers, who set up makeshift refugee camps. Official orders were issued to remove these African American civilians.

During the November 1864 expulsion, Federal soldiers forcibly expelled more than 400 women and children from the camp and then destroyed the refugee huts. Freezing temperatures and a winter storm resulted in more than one hundred of the displaced refugees dying of illness and exposure. A few weeks after the November expulsion, the U.S. Army reversed its policy toward African American enslaved refugees and began construction on the government-sponsored "Home for Colored Refugees" at Camp Nelson.

Lucy Carr Murphy (January 4, 1865 - February 24, 1910) was the wife of Isaac Burns Murphy. The couple married on January 24, 1883 in Lexington. In 1887, they purchased a grand home referred to as "The Murphy Mansion", located near East Third Street in Lexington, Kentucky. The brick house stood two stories tall on seven acres and featured an unusual rooftop observatory offering a view of the nearby Kentucky Association Racetrack.

The Murphy Mansion became a source of pride, particularly for African Americans, due to the fashionable social events hosted by the Murphys for both wealthy and less affluent community members. Local newspapers featured accounts of their all-day- and-night reception for jockey Anthony Hamilton and his fiancé as well as the celebration of Isaac and Lucy's tenth wedding anniversary.

Isaac Murphy died at the mansion in 1896. Over 500 people including Black and White dignitaries attended Isaac Murphy's funeral in Lexington. Over time, the house was lost to history. The Murphy Mansion was demolished in the 1930s and its precise location forgotten. There are no known photographs of the mansion.

Eli Jordan (June 1823 - September 22, 1908)

Excerpts from information authored by Yvonne Giles, Research Consultation, International Museum of the Horse.

Eli Jordan, born into slavery, spent his early years in Lexington, Kentucky. He lived on Fifth Street near the Kentucky Association Racetrack in East Lexington.

Archive records indicate that he married and had four daughters. From 1875 to 1877, Jordan was employed as a trainer with the stables of James T. Williams and Richard Owings. In 1878, Jordan and his family moved to Frankfort, Kentucky where he was hired as a trainer for Fleetwood Stable.

For over twenty-five years, Jordan oversaw the care, training, and racing of numerous outstanding Thoroughbreds, as well as the training of young stable boys and jockeys.

In 1891, Jordan provided information about Isaac Murphy, whom he had known since Isaac's early childhood. Jordan admired America Murphy's father, Green Murphy. Jordan's wife and Isaac's mother, America, were also close friends. America and Isaac lived in the Jordan household for a period when Isaac was very young.

Eli trained Isaac to become a highly successful jockey. Although Murphy began riding for Williams and Owings and Fleetwood Stables during the early part of his career, Jordan encouraged him to accept contracts from other owners. As a result, Isaac Murphy became the highest-paid sports star of his era.

Jordan's skills, knowledge, and devotion to horses kept him employed throughout his lifetime. His greatest achievements included training and supporting Isaac Murphy and Shelby Barnes, both of whom were inducted into the National Museum of Racing and Hall of Fame.

Eli Jordan died in Louisville, Kentucky and was buried in the Louisville Cemetery. Records confirm his internment, but his gravesite is unmarked. Although there are no existing photographs of Eli Jordan, his name and influence remain forever etched in the annals of Thoroughbred racing.

Elias Jackson "Lucky" Baldwin (April 3, 1828 – March 1, 1909) was described as "one of the greatest pioneers" of California business, a notable investor, and a real estate speculator during the second half of the 19th century. Baldwin earned the nickname "Lucky" due to his extraordinary good fortune in a number of business deals and at the racetrack. He built the luxurious Baldwin Hotel and Theatre in San Francisco and acquired vast tracts of land in Southern California, resulting in several neighborhoods and locations bearing his name. Baldwin founded the original Santa Anita Park racetrack on his estate (later closed, and re-opened again on the estate's land), breeding and racing some of the finest Thoroughbred race horses of his time.

Baldwin's horses won the American Derby at the Washington Park racetrack four times: Volante (1885); Silver Cloud (1886); Emperor of Norfolk (1888); and Rey el Santa Anita (1894). National Museum of Racing and Hall of Fame jockey Isaac Burns Murphy road three of Baldwin's four horses that won the American Derby and guided Baldwin owned horses to victories across the United States in the late 1800s.

Several places in California carry Baldwin's name, including the Baldwin Hills mountain range and the affluent Baldwin Hills neighborhood in South Los Angeles, the City of Baldwin Park, the Baldwin Stakes at Santa Anita, the Baldwin Village neighborhood, Baldwin Lake in the San Bernardino Mountains (near Baldwin's 1876 Gold Mountain Mine), Baldwin Beach at Lake Tahoe, and Baldwin Avenue in the San Gabriel Valley. His nickname also appears in the names of three pubs in Pasadena and Sierra Madre, including Lucky Baldwin's Pub in Pasadena, named in his honor.

The city of Sierra Madre now occupies land Baldwin once owned. A visitor to Santa Anita in 1886 remarked: "The ranch is a principality not unlike a Southern plantation before the Civil War, save that all the laborers are well-paid and well-fed." Baldwin was the largest employer and largest taxpayer in Los Angeles County at the time. Despite prevailing discrimination and racism in American society, Baldwin notably provided many jobs to African American workers, making headlines when he hired African Americans from North Carolina and paid for their train tickets to California.

T. THOMAS FORTUNE.

Newsman Timothy Thomas Fortune (October 3, 1856 – June 2, 1928) was an American orator, civil rights leader, journalist, writer, editor and publisher. He was the highly influential editor of the nation's leading Black newspaper *The New York Age* and a leading economist in the Black community. Fortune was a long-time adviser and friend to Booker T. Washington and edited Washington's first autobiography, *The Story of My Life and Work*. Fortune's philosophy of militant agitation on behalf of the rights of Black people laid one of the foundations of the Civil Rights Movement.

Timothy Thomas Fortune was born into slavery in Marianna, Jackson Country, Florida and started his education at Marianna's first school for African Americans after the Civil War.

Mostly self-taught before enrolling in Howard University in Washington D.C. in 1874, Fortune was initially admitted to study law but changed his major to journalism after two semesters, leaving school altogether in 1876 to begin work at *The People's Advocate,* a newspaper in Washington D.C. on February 21, 1878.

Fortune moved to New York City in 1879, becoming known over the next two decades as editor and owner of newspapers initially called *The Globe*, then *The Freeman*, and finally *The New York Age*.

On January 25, 1890, in Chicago, Fortune co-founded the militant National Afro-American League to fight injustices against African Americans authorized by law and tolerated by public opinion. The League played a vital role in setting the stage for the NAACP and other subsequent civil rights organizations to follow. Fortune was also the leading advocate of using "Afro-American" to identify his people. Since they are "African in origin and American in birth", he argued that the term most accurately defined them.

Architect Solon Spencer Beman (October 1, 1853 – April 23, 1914) was an American architect based in Chicago, Illinois, best known as the architect of the planned Pullman community and adjacent Pullman Company factory complex, as well as Chicago's renowned Fine Arts Building. Several of his other large commissions include the

Pullman Office Building, Pabst Building, and Grand Central Station in Chicago, as well as the Jockey Club at the original Washington Park racetrack in Chicago.

Working alongside Chicago architect Daniel H. Burnham, who was the director of the Chicago World Columbian Exposition of 1892-93, Solon designed several buildings. Solon also created the Blackstone Public Library, built in 1905 which was Chicago's first branch library. Solon's son, Spencer S. Beman was also an architect who worked with his father. The Art Institute of Chicago houses a collection of Solon and Spencer Beman's publications documenting architectural projects which also include more than ninety Christian Science churches.

Architect Daniel H. Burnham (September 14, 1846 - June 1, 1912) was an American architect and urban planner known most for his work in Chicago. He created the Roundhouse in Chicago's Washington Park, now part of the DuSable Museum of African American History. Burham originally designed the structure as stables in the 19th century along with a refectory and administrative headquarters for the South Park Commission. The Roundhouse was part of a larger park plan, including the South Open Green, a pastoral meadow.

Burnham was later selected as Director of Works for the 1892–93 World's Columbian Exposition. Considered to be the first example of a comprehensive planning document in the nation, the fairground featured grand boulevards, classical building facades, and lush gardens. Often called the "White City," it popularized neoclassical architecture in a monumental, yet rational Beaux-Arts style. As a result of the fair's popularity, architects across the U.S. were said to be inundated with requests by clients to incorporate similar elements into their designs.

General Philip Henry Sheridan (March 6, 1831– August 5, 1888) was a career Army officer and a Union general during the American Civil War. His military career was notable for his rapid promotion to major general and his close association with General-in-Chief, Ulysses S. Grant.

In 1871, Sheridan was present in Chicago during the Great Chicago Fire and coordinated military relief efforts. To calm the panic, Mayor Roswell B. Mason placed the city under martial law, and issued a proclamation appointing Sheridan in charge. Martial law was lifted within a few days due to lack of widespread disturbances. Although Sheridan's personal residence survived, his professional and personal papers were destroyed in the fire. When Chicago's Washington Park racetrack organized the American Derby in 1883, Sheridan served as its first president.

Charles Winter Wood (December 17, 1869 – June 9, 1953) was an American educator, actor and orator who graduated from Beloit College in Beloit, Wisconsin. He was the second head football coach at Tuskegee University in Tuskegee, Alabama and he held that position for four seasons, from 1897 until 1901. Wood spent 30 years at the Tuskegee Institute in the English and Drama departments.

The Freedman's Saving and Trust Company, known as the **Freedman's Savings Bank**, was a private savings bank chartered by the U.S. Congress on March 3, 1865, to collect deposits from the newly emancipated communities. Within seven years, the bank opened 37 branches across 17 states and Washington D.C., collecting funds from over 67,000 depositors. At its peak in 1872, the bank held assets worth more than $3.7 million in 1872 dollars, (approximately $80 million in 2021 dollars). However, its rapid growth was largely based on false claims and marred by mismanagement and fraud.

The bank failed in 1874 due to speculative loans issued by its White officials throughout its existence. Historians believe that the bank's collapse not only destroyed the savings of many African Americans, but also damaged their trust in financial institutions.

Solar Eclipse of 1879, Kentucky (August 7, 1879) was an annular solar eclipse and an event of significant national interest. The eclipse's central line, where annularity (the ring of fire) was most visible, passed through several towns in Kentucky. Many people traveled long distances to witness the event. Shelby College, located in Shelbyville, Kentucky, with its state-of-the-art telescope, became a central gathering point for astronomers and visitors during the eclipse.

Edward H. "Snapper" Garrison (February 9, 1868 – October 28, 1930) was an American jockey famous for his racing style—hanging back for most of the race and finishing at top speed to achieve thrilling victories. He rode Tenny against Isaac Murphy riding Salvator in what was known as "The Match Race of the Century" between a White rider and a Black rider. Garrison and Tenny lost the race by a nose, confirmed in a historical photograph by John C. Hemment.

Anthony Hamilton (July 5, 1886 - February 21, 1904) was born in Charleston, South Carolina and began his notable jockey career at age fifteen. Hamilton possessed natural talent with a rare balance of strength and finesse who demonstrated instinctive timing throughout his races. Hamilton won many of the most prestigious American races, including all three major New York handicaps.

Tony Hamilton and Isaac Murphy were close friends who trained and competed together. Isaac and his wife Lucy hosted a lavish engagement party for Tony and his fiancé at their home in Lexington, Kentucky. Isaac was asked to serve as Anthony's best man at the wedding on Jan. 22, 1891 in St. Louis.

Hamilton's other significant racing victories included the 1887 American Derby, consecutive wins at Monmouth Oaks in 1889 and 1890, the inaugural Gazelle Handicap in 1887 and five editions of the Twin City Handicap.

In the early 1900s, Hamilton achieved international success, winning major races in Vienna, Austria; Warsaw, Poland; Budapest, Hungry;

and Russia in 1904. Hamilton won the prestigious first race of the Polish Triple Crown.

John C. Hemment

Photographer John C. Hemment (January 28, 1862 - 1927) was an avid athlete and pioneering photographer, notably one of the first to capture close race finishes in both human and horse races. His innovative experiments with lenses and shutter speeds led to some of the first documented "photo-finishes". The John C. Hemment Photographic Collection contains over 5,200 black-and-white photographs from the late 19th and early 20th centuries emphasizing tracks in New York and Maryland and depicting track scenes, paddocks, horses, social gatherings and notable figures in Thoroughbred racing. The Keeneland Library in Lexington, Kentucky is home to the Hemment Photographic Collection.

The Ku Klux Klan commonly shortened to KKK or Klan, is an American Protestant-led Christian extremist, White supremacist, far-right hate group.

It was founded in 1865 during the Reconstruction era in the devastated Southern United States of America. Various historians have characterized the Klan as America's first terrorist group. Initially established by Confederate veterans opposing Reconstruction, the Klan assaulted and murdered politically active Black people and their White political allies in the South.

Federal law enforcement began actions against the Klan around 1871. The Klan consisted of numerous autonomous and secretive chapters across the Southern United States, whose members created their own distinctive, often colorful, costumes—including robes, masks and pointed hats—to intimidate and conceal their identities.

The Jim Crow laws were state and local laws introduced in the Southern United States in the late 19th and early 20th centuries that enforced racial segregation. "Jim Crow" is a pejorative term for an

African American. The last of the Jim Crow laws were overturned in 1965.

Formal and informal racial segregation policies were present in other areas of the United States as well, even as several states outside the South had banned discrimination in public accommodations and voting. Southern laws were enacted by White-dominated state legislatures to disenfranchise and remove political and economic gains made by African Americans during the Reconstruction era in American history.

In practice, Jim Crow laws mandated racial segregation in all public facilities in the states of the former slave states and in some others, beginning in the 1870s. Jim Crow laws were upheld in 1896 in the case of *Plessy v. Ferguson,* in which the Supreme Court laid out its "separate but equal" legal doctrine concerning facilities for African Americans. Moreover, public education had essentially been segregated since its establishment in most of the South after the Civil War. Companion laws excluded almost all African Americans from voting in the South and deprived them of any representative government.

Although in theory, the "equal" segregation doctrine governed public facilities and transportation, facilities for African Americans were consistently inferior and underfunded compared to facilities for White Americans. Far from equality, as a body of law, Jim Crow institutionalized economic, educational, political and social disadvantages and second-class citizenship for most African Americans living in the United States. After the National Association for the Advancement of Colored People (NAACP) was founded in 1909, it became involved in a sustained public protest and campaigns against the Jim Crow laws, and the so-called "separate but equal" doctrine.

The Jim Crow laws were overturned by the Civil Rights Act of 1964 and the Voting Rights Act of 1965. Southern state anti-miscegenation laws were overturned in 1967. The miscegenation laws were state-level laws that prohibited people of different races to legally marry.

Thoroughbred is a breed of horse developed specifically for racing against other horses. Thoroughbreds are known for their agility and running speed. They have been selectively bred for centuries for competitive spirit, and a natural desire to head to the front of a pack. Thoroughbred horses enjoy the act of running and competition, but do not like to be whipped into submission by a rider.

The Triple Crown of Thoroughbred Racing, commonly known as the **Triple Crown**, is a series of horse races for three-year-old Thoroughbreds, consisting of the Kentucky Derby, Preakness Stakes and Belmont Stakes. The three races were inaugurated in different years, the last being the Kentucky Derby in 1875.

The Triple Crown Trophy, commissioned in 1950 but awarded to all previous winners as well as those after 1950, is awarded to a horse who wins all three races and is thereafter designated as a Triple Crown winner. The races are traditionally run in May and early June of each year.

Churchill Downs is a horse racing complex in South Louisville, Kentucky that hosts the annual Kentucky Derby. It was named for Samuel Churchill, whose family was prominent in Kentucky for many years. The first Kentucky Derby and the first Kentucky Oaks were held in 1875. With the infield open, the capacity of Churchill Downs is roughly 170,000.

In addition to the track, clubhouse and stables, Churchill Downs also contains the Kentucky Derby Museum which focuses on the history of the Kentucky Derby and Churchill Downs. The museum also contains a number of exhibits exploring the training and racing of Thoroughbred horses. It includes a 360-degree cinema that shows the short film "The Greatest Race", a documentary about the Kentucky Derby. The museum is normally open year-round.

A Jockey Club in the 1800s was more than just a gathering of horse racing enthusiasts; it was an influential organization that shaped the development and regulation of the sport, combining regulatory functions with the social aspects of an exclusive club. Membership attracted affluent individuals, often those involved in horse breeding and racing.

The main goal of a Jockey Club was to regulate and promote horse racing, as well as maintain the breed registry for Thoroughbreds. Jockey Clubs also served as social clubs for their members, providing elegant clubhouses and opportunities for socializing and gambling. Women's roles were often limited to the social aspects of the races, such as attending as spectators or being relegated to separate "ladies' sections" in grandstands. The Kentucky Historical Society notes that women were not allowed to become licensed jockeys until 1968, following legal challenges and the passage of the Civil Rights Act.

"The Purse" in horse racing refers to the total prize money that is distributed to the owners of the horses that finish in the top positions of a race. Isaac Murphy was presented with a symbolic gold-embroidered silk purse for his win on Kingman in 1891. The Murphy gold purse is currently on display in the Kentucky Derby Museum in Louisville, Kentucky.

Saratoga Race Course is a Thoroughbred horse racing track located on Union Avenue in Saratoga Springs, New York. Opened in 1863, it is the oldest major sporting venue of any kind in the U.S. The racetrack is operated by the New York Racing Association.

Saratoga Race Course is a hallowed venue where Isaac Murphy displayed his supreme skills. Saratoga is where he won the 1879 Travers Stakes aboard Falsetto. That victory catapulted eighteen-year-old Murphy into the national spotlight, defeating Belmont Stakes winner, Spendthrift, and the famed White jockey, Edward Feakes.

The Saratoga racetrack is nicknamed the "Graveyard of Champions" because several of the most famous Thoroughbreds in history were defeated there; Man o' War (1919, the only defeat out of twenty-one starts), Gallant Fox (1930, Triple Crown Winner, defeated by a horse that was a 100-1 long shot), Secretariat (Triple Crown Winner, defeated in 1973), and American Pharoah (Triple Crown Winner, defeated in 2015).

The Sheepshead Bay Racetrack was an American Thoroughbred horse racing facility built on the site of the Coney Island Jockey Club at Sheepshead Bay in Brooklyn, New York. The racetrack was built by a group of prominent businessmen from the New York City area who formed the Coney Island Jockey Club in 1879. On June 19, 1880 the track hosted its first day of Thoroughbred racing. On June 25, 1890, it hosted the match race between Tenny and Salvator.

Salvator (1886–1909) was an American Hall of Fame Thoroughbred racehorse considered to be one of the best racers during the latter half of the 19th century. Salvator was owned by James Ben Ali Haggin. Unusual for the times, the dark chestnut with a large white blaze was born in 1886 in California. Haggin had made his money in the California Gold Rush of 1849 and was one the wealthiest men in America at the time. He introduced jockey Isaac Murphy to the horse and the two bonded.

Salvator was the winner by a nose of "The Match Race of the Century" in 1890, mounted by Hall of Fame jockey Isaac Murphy against "Snapper" Garrison riding Tenny, at Sheepshead Bay. This historic race was followed by race fans around the world, widely covered in the press and memorialized by color illustrations and a black and white "photo-finish" image by photographer John C. Hemment.

Falsetto (1876–1904) was an American Thoroughbred champion racehorse bred and raced by J. W. Hunt Reynolds of Lexington, Kentucky. Conditioned for racing by African American trainer Eli Jordan, as a three-year-old in 1879, Falsetto won four of his five starts and was the dominant horse of its age group in the United States. Under African American star jockey, Isaac Murphy, Falsetto came in second in the 1879 Kentucky Derby, but that same year won the Phoenix Hotel Stakes, the Clark Handicap and defeated the great Spendthrift, ridden by Edward Feakes in the Travers Stakes at Saratoga. Owner J. W. Hunt Reynolds died in September 1880 and Falsetto was sent to England. Upon his return to Kentucky, he retired and sired three Kentucky Derby winners as well as a Thoroughbred who came in second in the Kentucky Derby in 1908.

James Ben Ali Haggin (December 9, 1822 – September 12, 1914) was an American attorney, rancher, investor, art collector and a major owner and breeder in the sport of Thoroughbred horse racing. Haggin made a fortune in the aftermath of the California Gold Rush and was a multi-millionaire by 1880. He was well acquainted with Elias "Lucky" Baldwin.

Haggin was born in Kentucky, the eldest of eight children, and a descendant of one of the state's pioneer families. In San Francisco, Haggin built a large and impressive mansion on Nob Hill, which stood until the earthquake and fire of 1906. He decorated the walls of his sixty-one room mansion with an art collection that would eventually be housed in the California Haggin Museum. Along with other investors, Haggin had a silver mine in Park City, Utah, another silver mine in South Dakota and a copper company in Montana.

Haggin purchased the Rancho Del Paso horse farm near Sacramento, California in 1859. He made it one of the country's most important horse breeding and horse racing operations, with Haggin's Thoroughbreds racing from coast-to-coast. One of his champion horses was Salvator, who Isaac Murphy mounted in "The Match Race of the Century" in 1890 at Sheepshead Bay racetrack. In 1905, Haggin shifted his horse breeding to Elmendorf Farm in Kentucky. Haggin had acquired Elmendorf in 1897 and until his death in 1914, worked to develop it into the largest horse breeding operation of its era in the United States.

William DeWolf Hopper (March 30, 1858 – September 23, 1935) was an American actor, singer, comedian, and theatrical producer. A star of vaudeville and musical theater, he became best known for performing the popular baseball poem "Casey at Bat".

Although his parents intended for him to become a lawyer, Hopper did not have an interest in that profession. Hopper was called Willie as a child, and then Will or Wolfie, but when he set out on an acting career, he chose his more distinguished middle name as his stage name. It was modified to "DeWolf" because of the frequency that it was mispronounced "Dwolf".

A lifelong baseball enthusiast and New York Giants fan, he first performed Ernest Thayer's then-unknown poem "Casey at Bat" to the Giants and Chicago Cubs the day his friend, Baseball Hall of Fame pitcher Tim Keefe, had his record 19-game winning streak stopped, August 14, 1888. Hopper helped make the comic poem famous and was often called upon to give his colorful, melodramatic recitation, which he did about 10,000 times in his booming voice, reciting it during performances and as part of curtain calls, and at social gatherings. He released a recorded version on the phonograph in 1906, and recited the poem in a short film made in the Phonofilm sound-on-film process in 1923.

African Cemetery No. 2, also known as The Cemetery of Union Benevolent Society No. 2, is a cemetery that was established in the rural setting on the East side of Lexington, Kentucky. The cemetery was the first burial site of Isaac Murphy.

The cemetery also holds the remains of Oliver Lewis, who won the inaugural Kentucky Derby in 1875 and James "Soup" Perkins. In addition, other African Americans related to the horse industry and their family members are also buried in African Cemetery No. 2., many in unmarked and abandoned graves.

Freemasonry is a fraternal organization with a long history rooted in the medieval stonemasons' guilds. It's a system of self-improvement, offering opportunities for personal growth, fellowship, and charitable endeavors. The organization emphasizes moral principles, social responsibility, and the pursuit of knowledge and understanding.

Freemasonry, "colored groups" primarily refers to Prince Hall Freemasonry, a branch of Freemasonry that emerged historically due to discrimination faced by African Americans in mainstream Freemasonry. It became the oldest and largest African American fraternity in the United States in the late 1800s.

At the encouragement of trainer Eli Jordan, Isaac Murphy joined the Freemasonry and rose through the ranks of leadership, becoming the Second Senior Warden. His leadership position was at the Lincoln and Sardis Lodge in Lexington. This position is the second of the three principal officers of a lodge. Isaac's Freemasonry brothers organized the formalities of his burial in 1896.

The Leader; Lexington, Kentucky; February 17, 1896; Page 5 column 2.

LAID TO REST

The Burial of Isaac Murphy Took Place Sunday Afternoon.

Yesterday afternoon the funeral services of Isaac Murphy was held at his late home on East Third street, and afterward the body was buried with Masonic ceremonies at the colored cemetery. At the funeral services at the home, conducted by Rev. S. P. Young, of the First Baptist Church, there was a very large gathering of friends of the dead jockey. Among the number was Col. James E. Pepper, Judge James R. Jewell, H Eugene Leigh, S. C. Eyne, John B Rogers and others. The floral offerings were beautiful and included a wreath from Fred Taral, a large and beautiful horse shoe from Anthony Hamilton and R. Williams, double hearts from John Perkins, a horse shoe from Charles Anderson, and large offerings of lillies of the valley from Ed Corrigan, Col. L. P. Tarlton and Ed Brown.

The body was escorted to the cemetery by Sardis and Lincoln Lodges, colored Masons, and Bethany Commandery, Knights Templar, and a large number of sorrowing friends.

The Kentucky Horse Park is the current burial site of the remains of Isaac Murphy, after having been moved twice since his death. For over seventy years, Isaac Murphy was buried in an unmarked grave in the abandoned African Cemetery No. 2 on the East side of Lexington along with his wife, Lucy.

In 1967, after a long search, Isaac's remains were exhumed and re-buried at the Man o' War burial site, and then moved again, along with Man o' War to the Kentucky Horse Park before its opening in 1978.

Today, Murphy rests beneath an engraved headstone (installed in 2015) next to the Man o' War rotunda in gardens outside of the entrance to the Kentucky Horse Park. There is no admission required to view Isaac Murphy's gravesite.

In 2015, the Kentucky Horse Park also introduced interpretive panels near Isaac Murphy's gravestone. They include, "Isaac Burns Murphy," "African Americans in Racing," and "Kentucky's African American Horsemen," intended to share important but mostly forgotten stories of Black riders with park visitors.

The Isaac Murphy Memorial Art Garden in Lexington, Kentucky, is the first park in the U.S. to honor the legendary African American jockey. The garden is located on land once owned by Murphy at the intersection of East Third Street, Midland Avenue and Winchester Road and features art, a small outdoor classroom, and the trailhead for the Legacy Trail.

The Isaac Murphy Memorial Art Garden features a 16-foot-tall stainless steel sculpture titled "My Home is a Horse and Track" paying homage to the racing legend and the garden's namesake. The garden and art installation were intended to be part of the Blue Grass Community Foundation's effort to revitalize Lexington's East End, which was home to one of Lexington's first important racetracks and the African American horsemen who lived and worked in this section of Lexington.

Pellom McDaniels III (February 21, 1968 – April 19, 2020) was an American professional football player who was a defensive lineman in the National Football League (NFL). His football career history includes Philadelphia Eagles (1991), Birmingham Fire (1991-92), Kansas City Chiefs (1993-98) and the Atlanta Falcons (1999-2000). After his playing career, he became a professor and curator at Emory University.

As a distinguished professor and historian, Pellom published a book *The Prince of Jockeys* through University Press of Kentucky in 2013 and in paperback in 2018. *The Prince of Jockeys* served as an inspiration and resource for the development of the screenplay, *Riding for America* by Eddie and Nancy Heffernan and the YA adapted novel *Riding for America* by Nancy Hays.

19th Century Black Jockeys (May 1875 – May 1902)

Sixteen of the first twenty-eight Kentucky Derbies were won by Black jockeys. Of the fifteen riders in the inaugural 1875 Kentucky Derby, thirteen were African American.

Black Kentucky Derby Winners:

- **Oliver Lewis** (1875)

- **William Walker** (1877)

- **James Carter** (1878)

- **Garrett Lewis** (1880)

- **Babe Hurd** (1882)

- **Isaac Murphy** (1884, 1890, 1891)

- **Erskine Henderson** (1885)

- **Isaac Lewis** (1887)

- **Alonzo Clayton** (1892)

- **James "Soup" Perkins** (1895)

- **Willie Simms** (1896, 1898)

- **Jimmy Winkfield** (1901, 1902)

African American jockeys were a dominant force in horse racing during the late 19th century, but their presence in the sport declined significantly in the early 20th century due to racial discrimination and the rise of the Jim Crow laws.

Black riders that have competed during the last century in the Kentucky Derby include Henry King (1921), Marlon St. Julien (2000), Kevin Krigger (2013) and Kendrick Carmouche (2021). None of those riders finished close to the top of the field in placement.

Oliver Lewis (December 22, 1856 - January 30, 1924) was an African American jockey in Thoroughbred horse racing. On May 17, 1875, Lewis won the very first Kentucky Derby aboard Aristides at the Louisville Jockey Club which was later named Churchill Downs. Aristides trainer was Ansel Williamson, who was also an African American. The pair won the first Kentucky Derby by a reported two lengths, setting a new American record time for a mile-and-a-half race. Ten thousand spectators watched the race. Lewis was only 19 years old.

Lewis won three more races at the Louisville Jockey Club, riding Aristide in all of them. Lewis and Aristides also took second place in the Belmont Stakes, which is now the third race of the U.S. Triple Crown series. Lewis would never ride in the Kentucky Derby again. He changed professions, married, moved to Ohio and had six children.

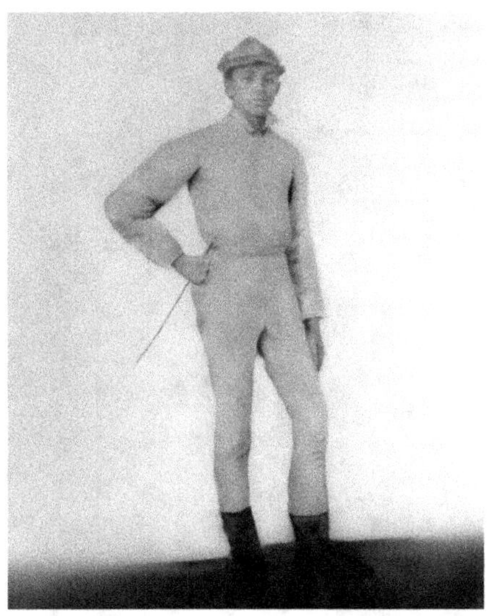

William Walker (1860 – September 20, 1933) was an American jockey. Born enslaved in Versailles, Kentucky, Billy Walker was the leading rider at Churchill Downs in the fall racing season of 1875–76 and the spring campaigns of 1876 through 1878.

Billy Walker rode Baden-Baden to victory in the 1877 Kentucky Derby. Walker made his fourth and final appearance in the 1896 Derby, finishing seventh. He retired that year but stayed in horse racing as a trainer. He was known to mentor Isaac Murphy. Billy Walker died in 1933 and was buried at the Louisville Cemetery. During the 1996 Kentucky Derby Week, Churchill Downs erected a headstone on Walker's previously unmarked grave with an epitaph outlining his career.

Willie Simms (January 16, 1870 – February 26, 1927) was an African American National Champion jockey in Thoroughbred racing and a National Museum of Racing and Hall of Fame inductee who won five of the races that would later become the U.S. Triple Crown series. He won the Kentucky Derby twice and back-to-back Belmont Stakes in 1893 and 1894 and the Preakness Stakes in 1898. He is the only African American jockey to win all three Triple Crown races. In 1895 Simms raced in England, where he became the first American jockey to win with an American horse in that country.

Shelby Barnes (June 1871 - January 6, 1908) was a Thoroughbred National Museum of Racing and Hall of Fame jockey who was trained by Eli Jordan. Barnes became established as a star in the Thoroughbred racing world in 1888. In that year, he achieved 206 wins (the most of any jockey that year) and a 32.9% win percentage (the highest of any jockey that year). While racing for Elias "Lucky" Baldwin's stables, Barnes won the Futurity Stakes (the biggest purse for any race that had been held to date). The race took place on Labor Day Weekend at Sheepshead Bay Racetrack in New York, drawing the largest attendance of any race that year.

By 1891, Barnes' racing career slowed down. He owned a farm in his hometown of Beaver Dam, Kentucky, and contemplated a return to racing that did not occur. Instead, he maintained partial ownership of a saloon in Columbus, Ohio. Barnes passed away in 1908 at the age of 37 due to tuberculosis.

James "Jimmy" Winkfield (April 12, c.1880–1882 – March 23, 1974) was a Thoroughbred jockey and a horse trainer from Kentucky. He won back-to-back Kentucky Derbys in 1901 and 1902. He was the last African American to ride a winner in the Kentucky Derby.

Winkfield was blackballed in the U.S. after dishonoring a contract to ride for an owner by agreeing to ride for a different owner, but he was offered a chance to race in Russia, where he quickly rose to fame. He won the Russian Oaks five times, the Russian Derby four times, the Czar's Prize on three occasions, and the Warsaw Derby twice. The Russian Revolution caused him to leave the country in 1917, and he moved to France where he resumed racing, scoring numerous wins. He retired as a jockey at age fifty having won more than 2,500 races, then began a second successful career as a horse trainer.

Alonzo "Lonnie" Clayton (January 4, 1876 – March 17, 1917) was an African American jockey in Thoroughbred horse racing. At age twelve, the diminutive Lonnie Clayton left home and made his way North to Chicago's Washington Park Racetrack where his brother Albertus was a jockey for Thoroughbred stable owner, Lucky Baldwin. Baldwin gave Lonnie a job as a stable hand and exercise rider. The following year, he moved to New Jersey where in 1890 the fourteen-year-old began his professional riding career. Alonzo holds the record as the youngest jockey to ever win the Kentucky Derby in 1892 at age fifteen.

As times became difficult for Black jockeys in America in the early 1900s, Clayton planned to join other Black jockeys riding in Europe. But no records have been found to confirm that he went there or competed in any international races. After legal troubles, he lived his last few years in California where he worked as a hotel bellhop. He died at age forty-one on March 17, 1917.

James "Soup" Perkins (February 28, 1879–August 10, 1911) was born in Lexington, Kentucky, the son of former slaves. James and his entire family were involved in horse racing, training, and working in the stables. Perkins was the second youngest jockey ever to win the Kentucky Derby and the winningest jockey in America in 1895. He was also very affluent, winning high-paying races and accumulating wealth from his earnings. Perkins was written about in newspapers throughout the United States and Canada.

Because his father worked in the stables, Perkins began working with horses at the age of nine. At eleven he began racing as a jockey. He received the nickname "Soup" for his well-known love of soup, which helped keep his weight down.

In 1895, Perkins rode Halma to victory in the Kentucky Derby, leading the race from wire to wire. That same year he had 762 mounts and won 192 races, the most wins of any jockey in America.

He died at the age of thirty-three from a massive heart attack while working in Hamilton, Ontario, Canada. His wife had his remains brought back to Lexington, where he was buried in African Cemetery No. 2. A historical marker was placed at his grave by a University of Kentucky Commonwealth Collaboratives Grant Young Equestrian Scholars Initiative.

Notable American Female Jockeys

Cheryl White (October 29, 1953 — September 20, 2019) was the first **African American** female horse racing jockey and the first woman to serve as a California horse racing steward. National newspapers covered her first start as a jockey, and she appeared on the cover of the July 29, 1971, issue of *Jet Magazine.*

White is credited with 226 wins in Thoroughbred racing, but her career also included Quarter Horse, Arabian, Paint, and Appaloosa racing. In total, White estimates that she won 750 races. As a Thoroughbred rider, White became the first woman to win two races on the same day in two states in 1971. She was also the first female jockey to win five races in one day, achieving this feat on October 19, 1983, at the Fresno Fair.

Diane Crump (born May 18, 1948) is an American jockey and horse trainer. Crump was the first female professional jockey (1969) and the first woman to ride in the Kentucky Derby (1970). The pioneer rider shattered the glass ceiling for women on the horse racing saddle. A year earlier, Diane became the first female professional jockey when she ran the Hialeah Park Racetrack in front of a crowd that was so hostile about a female competing that she needed a police escort to get on the track.

Julieann Louise Krone (born July 24, 1963) is a retired American jockey. In 1993, Krone became the first and only (and as of June 2025) female jockey to win a Triple Crown race when she captured the Belmont Stakes aboard Colonial Affair. In 2000, she became the first woman inducted into the National Museum of Racing and Hall of Fame. In 2003 she became the first female jockey to win a Breeder's Cup race. She has also been honored by induction into the National Women's Hall of Fame, Michigan Women's Hall of Fame, and Cowgirl Hall of Fame.

Krone was the only woman to win riding championships at Belmont Park, Gulfstream Park, Monmouth Park, The Meadowlands, and the Atlantic City Race Course. She made television appearances on *The Late Show with David Letterman*, *The Tonight Show with Jay Leno* and appeared on the cover of *Sports Illustrated* for the issue of May 22, 1989. In 1993 she received an ESPY Award as Female Athlete of the Year.

Anna Rose "Rosie" Napravnik (February 9, 1988) is a former American Thoroughbred horse racing jockey and two-time winner of the Kentucky Oaks. Beginning her career in 2005, she was regularly ranked among the top jockeys in North America in both earnings and total races won. By 2014 she had been in the top 10 by earnings three years in a row and was the highest-ranked woman jockey in North America. In 2012 she broke the total wins and earnings record for a woman jockey previously held by Julie Krone. Napravnik's fifth-place finish in the 2013 Kentucky Derby and third in the 2013 Preakness Stakes on Mylute are the best finishes for a woman jockey in those two Triple Crown races to date. She is the only woman to have ridden in all three Triple Crown races.

Donna Barton Brothers (born April 20, 1966) is a former jockey who won over 1,100 horse races and now covers horse racing and other equestrian sports for NBC Sports. She is most recognizable for her interviews with the winning jockeys from horseback after the Triple Crown and Breeders' Cup races. She is one of the most decorated female jockeys of her time, retiring in 1998 with 1,130 career wins. Brothers hails from a family of riders, including both of her siblings, as well as her mother who was, in 1969, one of the first women to be licensed as a jockey. She resides in Louisville, Kentucky and Saratoga Springs, New York.

Excerpts from 2011 Article entitled *The American Jockey 1865-1910* from the *Transatlantic American Studies Journal,* an International Publication printed in English and French.

Scholars have largely neglected the history of Thoroughbred racing in the United States even though it was among the most important American sports. The Sport of Kings drew estimated crowds in excess of 50,000 in the ante-bellum era, long before baseball or football had developed. Following the Civil War, racing boomed in the North, particularly in New York City, the site of such elite courses as Sheepshead Bay and Belmont Park. Prestigious Jockey Clubs ran those tracks, because they enjoyed gambling, the sociability at the tracks' elegant clubhouses, and the status membership provided. As recently as the 1950s and 1960s, horse racing was the number one spectator sport in the United States. However, it is currently struggling to survive due to international competition for the finest horses, and especially from competition for the gambling dollar from government-sponsored lotteries, legalized betting parlors, including sports wagering, computer gaming, and illegal enterprises.

There has been extensive literature published in America on professional baseball players, prizefighters, football players, and basketball players. However, historians have not thoroughly studied the occupation of the jockey. The conventional wisdom among bettors is that the best horse wins regardless of the rider. But during the 1800s, jockeys were not just along for the ride, but owners and fans alike recognized them for their skill, courage, and savvy as they guided, eased, and prodded their mounts to the winner's circle. Bettors increasingly chose their bets by the jockeys as much as the horses. In the 1880s, tracks began to post the names of jockeys together with the horses at the pool stands because some gamblers got more business if their clients knew the rider. Jockeys in this era were the highest paid athletes in North America.

There were at least 117 African American jockeys after the Civil War. They had a very high reputation for honesty and integrity. As one newspaper asserted in 1890, "They know that in the skill of their hands and in the alertness of their brains and eyes rests many a time the fate of fortunes, and they seldom abuse the confidence placed in them." *(Ashe 125; Trenton Daily True American, June 4, 1890, 3)*

An article in the *New York Herald* in 1889 was entitled, *Colored Jockeys Show the Way*. The preeminent African American jockey in the late 1880s, was Isaac Burns Murphy. According to L.P. Tarelton, the former owner of the Fleetwood Stables, "I have seen all the great jockeys of England and this country for years back…Isaac Murphy is the greatest of them all."

Isaac Murphy, Keeneland Library
Hemment Collection

America and Isaac Murphy's Legacy and Inspiration

There is a good reason why we chose to highlight America Murphy's story in *Riding for America* alongside Isaac's. Understanding the sacrifices America made during their pre-and post–Civil War journey is crucial. America's risks, determination, and strength helped build a better life for her son—on and off the racetrack. Isaac Burns Murphy became known as "The Prince of Jockeys" because he was raised by a mother who valued education, learning, and excellence in every task he undertook.

Isaac grew up at a pivotal time in American history. His father, Jerry Burns, fought in the U.S. Colored Troops and died during the Civil War. Not only did Isaac experience fleeing slavery on the Tanner farm with his mother, but it is believed that mother and son also endured being cast into the wilderness as refugees from Camp Nelson by the Union Army during the winter of 1864, when Isaac was only three years old. The Army forcibly removed Black refugees from Camp Nelson at least eight times that year. America and Isaac were likely part of the initial 400 women and children expelled from the camp during a winter storm. As a result, more than 102 people died.

The great solar eclipse of 1879, the collapse of Freedman's Bank, and the first use of photo-finish photography were also historically significant moments in Isaac's lifetime. The fact that Isaac was literate made a profound difference in both his life and career. At the time of his birth, enslaved people were not permitted to read or write. There were no schools or libraries for Black children in America until after the Civil War. The books Isaac acquired and read as a child, teenager, and adult helped him escape in his mind during times of extreme difficulty. Reading calmed his nerves and inspired him. The scripture he read grounded him in faith and gave his life purpose. One of Isaac's goals was to build a personal library, and he accomplished that goal at the mansion he shared with his wife, Lucy, on East Third Street in Lexington.

Thanks to his mother America's exemplary teaching and his own self-education and determination, Isaac spoke to the press with clarity and dignity. Toward the latter part of his career, he was able to write his own advertising listings so his services could be marketed to wealthy horse owners—and he could command maximum pay as a top jockey. Journalists who studied his career noted that Isaac was "a great copy" when interviewed for race coverage. He was an excellent listener, could explain his racing strategy clearly, and conversed with highly educated men as one of their peers.

Isaac was also a different kind of competitor. His closest friend, Anthony Hamilton, was another Black jockey and his rival on the racetrack. Even though horse racing is an individual sport with only one winner in each race, Isaac and Anthony did not see their relationship that way. Rather than letting competition compromise their friendship, they supported each other with humor, teamwork, and shared training. They celebrated victories and defeats together and made history both jointly and individually. Isaac was asked to be the best man at Anthony's wedding—a grand celebration held in St. Louis.

Isaac had a strong connection to the city of Chicago. Records show that he owned a second home in the Windy City with his wife, Lucy, and Isaac won four of the first five American Derbies held on Chicago's South Side. Although the Washington Park racetrack has long since been demolished, the Roundhouse, which now houses the DuSable Museum of African American History, was once part of the original horse stables where Isaac and Tony Hamilton housed, groomed, and raced Thoroughbreds.

After Isaac's death, as racial tensions escalated and Black jockeys were denied access to the best mounts, Anthony Hamilton and other Black riders found success overseas, where they could compete without the racial prejudice that eventually led to the exclusion of Black jockeys from all Jockey Clubs in America during the Jim Crow era. Although Black jockeys were the originators of horse racing in America—winning sixteen of the first twenty-eight Kentucky Derbies—they virtually disappeared from the sport by the end of the 19th century.

Isaac's upright riding style (as opposed to the crouched position common today) and his rare use of a whip also made him unique. He respected horses and understood that they loved to race, but beating them didn't make them run faster. He trained his mounts thoughtfully, coaxing them to perform at their best. From Eli Jordan, he learned to give horses just enough margin to win without overextending or hurting them.

Eli Jordan, who managed stables and trained horses for over twenty-five years, was a surrogate father to Isaac. He taught Isaac how to ride and succeed, and gave his blessing when Isaac left his stable to work for Lucky Baldwin and other wealthy owners—so he could build the most successful and profitable career possible in Thoroughbred racing.

Eli was indisputably one of the greatest coaches of young jockeys in racing history. Though no known photograph of him exists, and his resting place is an unmarked grave, his legacy endures through the lives he shaped. Eli's teachings—on efficiency, pacing, compassion, and proper horse care—often determined the difference between winning and losing. More importantly, his wisdom made him a winner in life. Eli fathered four biological daughters and helped raise two jockeys—Isaac Murphy and Shelby Barnes—who would later be inducted into the National Museum of Racing and Hall of Fame.

Isaac is buried at the Kentucky Horse Park in Lexington, in a grave and memorial adjacent to the large rotunda honoring Man o' War. While his resting place includes an impressive marker and notable plaques, it is unfortunate that his beloved wife, Lucy, as well as America Murphy, and many other Black jockeys, trainers, and groomsmen, remain in unmarked graves at African Cemetery No. 2 in Lexington.

Isaac's famous gold purse from his final Kentucky Derby win in 1891 on a horse named Kingman is now on display at the Kentucky Derby Museum. Kingman was the first Thoroughbred co-owned by an African American—Dudley Allen—who was also born into slavery. Today, visitors to the Derby Museum in Louisville, Kentucky, can explore an expanded exhibit honoring early Black jockeys. With a special request, guests can enjoy a personal tour of this exhibit guided by a trained host.

Isaac Burns Murphy was a sports superstar with class, sophistication, and impeccable integrity. His life exemplifies perseverance and triumph against unimaginable odds. Isaac was a great son, pupil, mentor, husband, friend—and a great American. He deserves to be remembered and celebrated as one of the most extraordinary sports heroes in U.S. history.

Study Guide

The major messages we want students to take away include:

1. Black jockeys were the originators of horse racing in America. Thirteen of the fifteen jockeys who raced in the first Kentucky Derby were African American. Sixteen of the first twenty-eight Kentucky Derbies were won by Black riders.
2. Isaac Murphy, the son of formerly enslaved parents, is arguably the greatest jockey of all time. His overall record remains unmatched.
3. Washington Park in Chicago was built to house a racetrack, Jockey Club, and stables for Thoroughbred racing. It was the site of the first American Derby, which at the time offered the highest winning purse in U.S. horse racing history.
4. The Roundhouse at the current DuSable Museum of African American History in Chicago houses the original stables from Washington Park.
5. Fort Nelson was a critical Civil War site in Kentucky. It was where enslaved men could enlist in the Union Army to fight for their freedom. Isaac's father joined the United States Colored Troops there. It is believed that America and Isaac sought asylum at Camp Nelson after fleeing the Tanner farm.
6. In the story *Riding for America,* Isaac and his mother became refugees in the wilderness near Lexington, Kentucky, after being expelled from Fort Nelson by the Union Army. Isaac was just a toddler. That winter, 102 Black refugees lost their lives.

7. Eli Jordan, a Black trainer, was one of the greatest horsemen in American history. He served as a surrogate father, mentor, and teacher to Isaac Murphy, imparting lessons in discipline, science, pacing, efficiency, and observation.

8. Freedman's Bank was created after the Civil War to help Black families save and invest. It went bankrupt in 1874, causing many Black Americans to lose their life savings.

9. Isaac Murphy won one of the first photo-finish races in American sports history. The race featured Isaac riding Salvator against Snapper Garrison on Tenny. Isaac won by a nose. The photo was taken by John C. Hemment.

10. Isaac was a sportsman who did not use the whip to force speed. He treated horses with kindness and relied on intellect and strategy to win races.

11. Isaac never accepted bribes or placed bets. He competed fairly and encouraged others, including his best friend and rival Anthony Hamilton, to do the same.

12. In *Riding for America*, Isaac found inspiration and comfort in reading, especially literature by William Shakespeare.

13. Isaac's golden purse from his final Kentucky Derby win in 1891 on Kingman is on display at the Kentucky Derby Museum in Louisville. Kingman was the first horse co-owned by an African American, Dudley Allen. There wasn't another Black co-owner of a Kentucky Derby Thoroughbred until after the year 2000.

14. Isaac Murphy is buried in Lexington, Kentucky, at the Kentucky Horse Park, next to the grave of Man o' War, the most famous racehorse in U.S. history.

15. The Isaac Murphy Award is given annually to the jockey with the highest winning percentage.

16. Isaac and other Black jockeys are featured in a permanent exhibit at the Kentucky Derby Museum.

17. Much of Isaac's success was made possible by the strength and sacrifice of his mother, America Murphy.

18. Due to racism and Jim Crow laws, Black jockeys were systematically excluded from American racing after the 19th century. There have been very few African American jockeys in Stakes races during the last one hundred twenty years.

19. Anthony Hamilton, a Black jockey and close friend of Isaac, trained and competed alongside him. Isaac was asked to be the best man at Anthony's wedding, showing the depth of their friendship despite their rivalry.

20. Several Black jockeys, including Anthony Hamilton, found success racing in Europe after being pushed out of American racing due to racial discrimination.

Other related materials and projects in development:

Website: www.RidingforAmericaDrama.com

Riding for America, Feature Film Screenplay by Eddie and Nancy Heffernan

Riding for America, Stage Play by Eddie and Nancy Heffernan

Riding for America, Picture Book by Nancy Hays and Jan Spivey Gilchrist (ages 5-9)

Riding for America, Student Classroom and Community Program (2025 Illinois Arts Grant Recipient)

Contact: Nancy Hays Entertainment, Inc., nancyhaysentertainment@gmail.com, 773-383-8984

www.ingramcontent.com/pod-product-compliance
Lightning Source LLC
Chambersburg PA
CBHW060347310726